ACKNOWLEDGMENT

To my first college friend
Chevette Madden
for being my Editor in Chief
of both novels!

DEDICATION

This book is dedicated

To

Tiana Overton-Allah

For being the greatest supporter of my books

AuthorHouse™
1663 Liberty Drive
Bloomington, IN 47403
www.authorhouse.com
Phone: 1 (800) 839-8640

Published by AuthorHouse 03/12/2018

ISBN: 978-1-5462-2758-8 (sc)
ISBN: 978-1-5462-2757-1 (e)

Library of Congress Control Number: 2018901495

Print information available on the last page.

Every
"I Love You"
ISN'T TRUE
Part II

RaSheeda McNeil

authorHOUSE®

My Mama always said that every smile isn't real and every *"I love you"* isn't true.

PROLOGUE

"9-1-1...What is the address of your emergency? Do you need fire, medic, or police?"

"This is..." I made up in my mind to tell the truth, the whole truth, and nothing but the truth, but the two small red dots that suddenly appeared, one on my chest and the other on my head, caused me to rethink my current situation. I tried to dial 9-1-1 on my cell that I got back off of Seth's body. I looked directly at the two shooters, as if they weren't pointing guns, showing compliance. They knew that I had a change of heart by the current expression on my face.

As the operator kept repeating, "Fire, police or medic?" I pressed the end button on the phone disconnecting from the 9-1-1 operator.

I kept thinking about all the bodies lying in pools of fresh blood. I knew that I could become an accomplice to a crime and not just any crime, murder. Not just any murder, the murder of my captain, the man I used to sleep with, and he is so sadistic there is no telling what he planted for me to go down just in case the tables turned. I kept thinking to myself, *how did I get here? Why me? Can I even trust these people? Can I even trust myself now?*

Knowing I was screwed either way, I reluctantly said, "You two get the legs and I'll get the arms."

"We are going to have to burn the body this time. We can't leave any room for mistakes," one of the shooters said.

I replied sending a deadly look, "No shit Sherlock. If we leave it up to any of you, we all will be in jail."

"You're right. We can't even argue with you about that," one said, while the other agreed nodding their head. To my surprise they both started laughing but then the laughing abruptly stopped.

CHAPTER 1

Adrianna

"Run, Bitch, before I change my mind," Diamond said as she stood there with tears in her eyes, holding a smoking gun. She was too much of a boss to let a tear drop. She had perfect makeup and flowing, romance curled hair hanging flawlessly over her shoulders and down her back. She was gorgeous no matter what face she made. She refused to let me or anyone else see her cry. Flashbacks of me washing her hair, while she was recovering from me knocking her into my fiancés' grave, ran through my mind. I could see in her eyes that she was reflecting on all the fun we'd had double-dating, going to the Beyoncé concerts, and just sitting around having movie nights and cooking each other's favorite dishes for dinner. I knew she was thinking about the times I'd washed her hair when she couldn't wash her own and helped bathe her and put lotion on her until she was able to do it herself. Most importantly, she remembered the thrill we both got being boss bitches in the drug game, which was usually meant only for niggas to run. When we met with other bosses, when they found out that our set was run by two fine-ass bitches, the looks on their faces were priceless every time.

My house had become her house. Her all-white Chanel pantsuit had bloodstains all over it. She didn't blink or even look at Darnelle's body when it thumped onto the hardwood floor as it fell over. Blood was forming red stains on the chest of his black-and-white tuxedo. His mouth was full of blood, and I had to admit that both of us were full of shit. She was giving me a break, but I knew that this was far from over. I got up off of my knees but didn't move from that spot. I knew that at any moment, she would shoot me if I made the wrong move. I looked down at my left leg and realized it was shaking. I was so busy trying to control my bladder that I didn't notice that my hands and palms were sweating. Any moment now, someone from the wedding party was going to enter the room and demand to know what had happened. I didn't want to explain to my sister Charisma that I'd been fucking her fiancé. I didn't want to have to explain that when I was giving him head on their wedding day, the bitch who'd killed him had done so partially because he'd tried to blackmail her to fuck her. I didn't want to see Charisma's face when she found out he'd told Diamond that if she didn't have a ménage à trois with he and I, he would turn over the drug and murder evidence on her—the evidence I had provided him with when I thought Diamond was in on her brother Sly's attempt to kidnap me and rape me. Only when Diamond shot her brother in the head while he was on top of me had I realized that she had nothing to do with his foolishness. She had saved my life, but I wanted to take hers as payback for sleeping with a nigga who was supposed to be mine but clearly only cared about himself. I had Bossman's heart, but clearly, Diamond had his mind. We had gone from being enemies to being friends and now back to being enemies all in one year.

"Wait!" I said to Diamond, hoping she wouldn't change her mind and just shoot me.

"Give me the gun," I whispered, holding my hand out.

"Bitch, is you stuck on stupid? Why would I give you the gun—so you can shoot me?" Diamond said with a serious look on her face.

I reassured her by saying, "No, no. We can say it was self-defense. They will believe me. I can tell my sister that he tried to rape me, and I shot him. So give me the gun, so I can fire it. That way, I can have my fingerprints on it with gun residue on my hands." She still wasn't budging, but she heard people running up the steps from the wedding party, so she understood time was limited. "Diamond, you saved my life. I fucked up. I don't want you to go to jail over this nigga. Charisma is a lawyer. After I tell her what he tried to do, she will never let me see a day in jail." I could see her thinking about it. She loosened her grip on the diamond-studded nine. I quickly grabbed it and fired twice. I fired up into the ceiling and then dropped the gun just before Charisma, my father, and Rashad came flying into the room.

CHAPTER 2

Jullian

A hoe was going to be a hoe no matter what. That was why I kept hoes out of my circle. However, you had no choice about keeping a hoe around when that hoe was family. That was called a family hoe. Every family had one. If you thought your family didn't, then you were probably the hoe. You just had to remember the golden rule: never let a hoe be around your man alone under any circumstances. If he was in the kitchen during Thanksgiving dinner and the family hoe was there, then you were in the kitchen. If your man was still up, chatting it up with the boys, on Christmas Eve, then you were still up on Christmas Eve. If he woke up to use the family bathroom, then you woke up and acted as if you had to use the bathroom. If you gave the family hoe no breathing room, he wouldn't smell her scent. You shouldn't even tell him that she's the family hoe, because curiosity would kill the cat. Then you would have to kill him. Doing these things would not necessarily stop your man from cheating, but it would stop that man from cheating with that hoe. If a man decided to cheat, you, as the woman, got more credibility if he cheated with an outside hoe. You got zero respect if he cheated with the family hoe, because you knew she was a hoe from the beginning, and you let your man be around her unattended. If the hoe wins, it's because you let her win.

Boom! Boom! Boom! Boom! "Jullian, are you in the dressing room reading that book? Bitch, we hungry!" Adrianna said with frustration, while shaking her head.

"Bitch, you need to be reading it. The chapter I just read, *Why Hoes Be Winning,* was dedicated to you," I said, being condescending. Adrianna slipped up and told me all about her and Darnelle. After daddy stopped speaking to me - after catching his girlfriend, Chantal, and I on the kitchen counter - I confided in my sister

Adrianna. I couldn't tell my oldest sister Charisma because she would never look at me the same way again. She was too much of a lady and too much of a daddy's girl to ever forgive me. Adrianna kept my secret and she decided to tell me hers. She was fucking Charisma's fiancé all the way up to the day of the wedding. That was so foul, but I'm not going to cut her off. For one, that's my sister. For two, keep your friends close and keep them hoes closer. I can't cut her off because she is family. However, like the book says, *I know she is the family hoe so I just know not to leave my man or my woman around her.*

I knew I was wrong for falling for my father's younger girlfriend, but Chantal caught me at a vulnerable time. She pursued me right after losing the love of my life, West, to the game. He and Bossman, which was Adrianna's boo, ran the drug game in Charlotte before they were both killed execution style. I never even thought about another woman's pussy. She knew that I was vulnerable, grieving, and lonely. When my father, Warren, became ill I had him and Chantal come live with me. The mansion that West left me was big enough. Chantal kept me company and we became really close friends. I agreed to take care of him while she worked. She ran her own massage spa. She snuck in my room while I was sleeping one night, opened my legs, and began to suck my clit. I thought I was dreaming. I called West's name out in my sleep then I realized it wasn't West - it was Chantal. By the time I realized it was her, I was cumming. She let me cum all in her mouth and she just slurped it all up like a pro. I was ashamed, embarrassed, shocked, and satisfied all at the same time. I tried to stop sleeping with her but I just couldn't. It was as if she could read horny on my face. I didn't want to sleep with another man so soon after West's death and she used that to her advantage.

After my father caught us that day, I ended things with her. I told her that I never wanted to see her again. To my surprise she showed up at Charisma and Darnelle's wedding! She begged me to come back to her but I couldn't. Ever since then she has been writing me love letters, calling me, and showing up at my home at least once a week to express her love. I would have called the police but I knew she wasn't dangerous. It was just getting on my nerves so I'd decided to move.

Adrianna and I went shopping while the movers were moving my stuff. I made sure they moved it while Chantal had an appointment with a client at the spa. Adrianna had her friend Misha schedule an appointment with Chantal at the spa to make sure she was busy as I moved. I didn't need her showing up to my new spot. I missed our friendship but I didn't want the relationship. I had a lesbian encounter but I didn't consider myself gay. I was just fucked up in the head at the time.

After a loss, be careful who you let in your circle. Hoes know when you are vulnerable. That's how hoes be winning, according to Ms. Jones, the author of *Hoes Be Winning*. They catch you when you're sleeping. In my case, literally! *Ring…Ring… Ring…*Looking down at my cell phone my sister immediately knew it was my ex fling, Chantal, calling me for the ninth time today. I can't believe I slept with my father's then girlfriend. "Looks like I have to change my number again. This is getting tiring."

Adrianna proudly said, "As of now, you sleeping with his then girlfriend overrides me sleeping with Darnelle. I might be the family hoe but right now you are the top family hoe." We both fell out laughing. We laughed so hard that the mere look at each other caused us to laugh again.

"After we eat at The Cheesecake Factory let's go by and see the baby." The look on Adrianna's face told me that she was happy about that. "Let me call to see if Charisma and Rashad are at home," I said while following the waiter to our table. We had so many shopping bags in our hands from Macy's, Nordstrom, and Neiman Marcus that it was ridiculous. We had to place some of the bags under the table because there wasn't any room left beside us in our booth.

Rashad is such a good man. He and Charisma are so happy. He is raising Jordan like his own. He said since Darnelle is dead and he ended up marrying Charisma, on her and Darnelle's wedding day, that he might as well be the daddy. Charisma was so pissed at Adrianna and Darnelle that she almost dragged Rashad down the altar. He didn't mind because he was there to break up the wedding anyway. He wanted to marry Charisma and be the father that Dream never had. Dream was the child that Rashad and Charisma had when Charisma was a teen. Our mother sent her away for nine months making her vow not to tell Rashad. After Charisma and

Kendra, Rashad's wife at the time, were involved in a car accident, both families collided at the hospital. Rashad saw Dream and the rest was history. He was angry at Charisma for a while for not telling him about Dream but he couldn't stay mad. They have been living happily ever after ever since.

Charisma distanced herself from Adrianna but decided not to stay mad at her because at the end of the day Adrianna was still her sister and Darnelle was still a dog. It just made her decision to marry Rashad easier because that's what her heart wanted anyway. Charisma didn't know the full story but still helped us cover up Darnelle's murder.

She admitted that she always thought Darnelle was screwing around but would never mention it until she found proof. She never thought it would be her own flesh and blood. She smelled the truth in the air, between Adrianna and Darnelle, the moment she entered the room at the church. Charisma felt so bad about cheating on Darnelle with Rashad that she decided to finally have sex with him, just one time, for the first time, before the wedding. Darnelle felt so bad about cheating on Charisma, with her sister that he got her pregnant, that night, on purpose. He knew it would be harder for her to leave him, if she ever found out about him and Adrianna, if he was both her baby's father and her husband. However, his feelings changed towards Charisma when he found out about her and Rashad from drunken Mr. Joseph, our mother's ex. Mr. Joseph was so drunk at Darnelle's bachelor party the night before the wedding, all because my mother and father got back together, that he told Darnelle about the conversation between Charisma and our mother. In that conversation, Charisma told mom all about her and Rashad. She had no choice because mama figured out that she was pregnant. She put two and two together at Bossman's funeral. Of course, Charisma didn't buy Adrianna's story that Darnelle tried to rape her nevertheless; she didn't want her sister to go to jail so she played along. In addition, she was a couple of months pregnant and she didn't need the extra stress. It didn't hurt that Diamond, supposedly a former client of Darnelle's, came out to say that he attempted to rape her, too, one day at his office. Diamond testified that she didn't have the strength to come clean until she saw Adrianna's story on the news. I have to give them bitches credit. They had the story on lock but Charisma was no fool. While everyone was upstairs inside the church or outside wondering how in the world someone got killed at the wedding, Charisma and Rashad were in the sanctuary getting married with Dream and I as the witnesses. Charisma had a heart of gold but once she found out that you screwed her she had no love for you. I mean, anybody that marries another man while her fiancé is upstairs dead and the body isn't even cold yet, is cold-blooded. It was just a ceremonial wedding. They would make it official on paper later. Why waste the cake? *These bitches are crazy,* I thought to myself as we pulled up to Charisma's house. I looked at Adrianna as she was getting out of the car and thought to myself, *I have to keep one eye open at all times with these hoes.*

CHAPTER 3

Adrianna

I was nervous as hell about seeing Charisma for the first time since she found out I slept with her dead fiancé. Riding past Lake Norman on the way to our sister's house was awkward considering Boss, West, Diamond, and I had bodies there. As we pulled into Charisma's private road to her driveway I immediately felt uncomfortable. "Something doesn't seem right sis. Why did she move to a house that no one can see from the street?" I said, looking from side to side through the trees that were on both sides of the road before pulling up to the house.

"You are just having flashbacks from your old life Adrianna or perhaps you're just nervous from watching the movie *Wrong Turn* last night. Girl you know that movie had you shook," she said laughing.

"I'm a Boss Jullian. I don't get shook. I shoot." She knew I was dead serious too. A minute later Jullian was already out the car looking at me like, *Bitch hurry up!* As I applied my lip gloss one more time in the car mirror I noticed a candy apple red Corvette ease up behind us and park. When I saw Jullian freeze up I immediately cocked my nine and jumped out the car.

"Jullian, I just need a minute to talk to you face to face. Please just give me a minute," Chantal pleaded as she was getting out of the car.

As beautiful as she was, she looked as if she hadn't slept in days. Her hair was in a messy ponytail and she had on a loose T-shirt with pajama pants. I placed my nine back in my purse since it was only Chantal. I could use my hands if necessary. Stepping in front of Jullian, I asked, "Sis do you want me to take care of this for you?"

"No, I'm good sis." Her eyes never left Chantal.

Charisma opened her front door with my niece Dream right behind her. Charisma walked out onto the porch with her eyebrow raised. Immediately, she picked up on the vibe. Looking directly at Chantal, she asked firmly, "Is there a problem?" Then Dream said, "Yes, Aunties, is there a problem?" They looked at me and gave me that look that said, *No matter what, the Banks sisters stick together.* I looked back at them and grinned, but not long enough to let Chantal see it. Jullian ushered us to go inside so that she could speak with Chantal alone. Charisma opened her arms for me to hug her. It felt so good to hug my big sister again. Before entering the house I told Jullian that we were only a scream shot away if she needed us.

"Dang she doesn't get tired, huh?" Dream said, as we walked in the house. "Mama told me that she has been stalking Auntie Jullian." We just laughed. Rashad wasn't home so it was just us and the kids.

Dream was so pretty. She had on a cute black BeBe shirt with nicely fitted jeans that showed her shape perfectly. Running track gave her a body that most young girls would die for. She looked like a dream. Aunt Diane raised her very well, too. I was so happy to see her and my sister moving forward as mother and daughter. Dream has such a forgiving heart and Charisma is just a good person anyway. "Dream, congratulations on your full scholarship to Harvard. As much trouble as we get into, I might need you," I said jokingly, but so serious at the same time.

"Not as much trouble as you get into," Charisma said, stressing the *you* in her sentence. We all laughed again. Logging into her Facebook page on her tablet, Dream said, "My ultimate goal is to be a judge."

"Jordan is sleep sis, let me go wake him up," Charisma said, as she walked down the hallway to his bedroom.

Dream suddenly looked at me with relief and she said, "Good, she is gone. Mama is cool but she is still my Mama. This situation requires Auntie."

"What's up?" I asked Dream, looking at her with a face that said, *no one better be messing with my niece.*

"Auntie, I never start it but I will finish it real quick. This one girl keeps writing negative things about me on the Internet ever since I started dating her ex. She swears someone wants her man. I'm too focused on books and my future coins to be worried about a dude. Besides, he is three years older than I am. He is officially grown. She keeps throwing shade but never mentions me directly. I'm about two seconds from responding. I just don't want to tarnish my reputation because I have worked so hard to represent our family."

I was flattered that my niece came to me. I had to give her the best advice she ever heard. I lifted up her head by her chin so that we could look at each other in the eyes. Then I said, "Sometimes you have to leave lames to do the lame stuff that they do. We don't throw shade on Facebook; we shoot bullets in real life. Ignore her until she is ready to throw some hands." I could tell that she got the answers that she needed.

"Auntie!" Jordan called out with his hands out for me to pick him up. I picked him up and hugged him while spinning around in a circle. The fact that he called me Auntie meant she talked about me. That made me feel good inside.

"I show him pictures of us all the time." Charisma said, smiling with her eyes.

We were so in love with the moment that we forgot that Jullian was outside – until we heard someone laying on a car horn like a maniac. We ran outside and to our surprise Jullian and Chantal were fighting inside Jullian's car. We believe in fighting one-on-one, but Chantal was getting the best of Jullian. It was only because of the way she was positioned. Chantal was outside of the car pulling Jullian, who was in the driver's seat, through the driver's car window. My first reaction was to go back into the house quickly and get my gun out of my purse. *I swear I'm too cute to get dirty*, I said to myself, as I went full speed towards the car in my red bottoms. I have goons to get dirty but this situation was different. *Oh, so I thought.* This was about to be the first opportunity for Dream to witness us unfiltered, raw, and uncut.

Just before I reached them, Jullian pushed the door opened so hard it made Chantal fall to the ground. Then my sister jumped out the car like the Incredible Hulk yelling, "Bitch you got me fucked up!" That was the moment I realized she no longer needed my help and that things were about to go from 0-100… real quick! I saw her lift up her blue Timberland boot on her right foot and I knew what was coming next. She began to stomp Chantal like Larenz Tate stomped that dude in *Menace to Society*. After blood came out of Chantal's mouth I thought Jullian would stop, but to my surprise she kept going.

I heard Charisma behind me saying, "Dang sis, you beating her like she stole something." Charisma and I began to laugh but Jullian was still on 100. Chantal was trying to get up to go to her car but Jullian kept kicking her in her stomach, side, and everywhere else.

"Let her go sis," Charisma said, grabbing Jullian's arms. That allowed Chantal to crawl away to her car and get in.

Jullian angrily jerked away from Charisma saying, "No fuck that! She threatened me and said that if she couldn't have me then no one could! She tried to choke me to death in the car!"

Evenly surprised and with confused faces we both simultaneously asked, "She said what?!"

Then Charisma said, "Oh well then, carry on."

By the time she finished her sentence Chantal had jumped back out of her car with a .32 in her hand, aiming it at us, waving it from side-to-side. With a crazy look in her eyes she said, "I never meant for it to go this far. I was just trying to talk to you Jullian. I just want you to hear me out. I've been dying inside without you. You are the first woman I've ever loved. How dare you keep ignoring me like I meant nothing to you!" She grabbed Jullian by the waist while pointing the gun at Jullian's head. Chantal kissed her on her neck, saying, "I love you. I never stopped. Did you ever love me baby?"

With a straight face Jullian firmly said, "No." Charisma must have left her gun in the house, too, because I knew she would have pulled it out. We were screwed. I could tell that Chantal had completely lost it! Charisma tried to walk closer to them with her palms facing out to say she wasn't a threat. "Stay right there or I will shoot. I have nothing left to lose, Charisma. Your sister is my everything. Your father went back to your mother, and my twin Kendra moved out of state for her job after you took her husband Rashad away, Charisma." Then she said softly, "All I have is Jullian." She then let Jullian go by pointing the gun at her own head. Jullian didn't even turn around to look but you could tell she knew what Chantal was doing.

"No Chantal! Please don't do this," Charisma begged. "Help me talk to her Adrianna," she said trying to recruit me into the conversation. Jullian walked past me to enter Charisma's house still not looking back at Chantal.

"Do I look like a counselor? We have kids in the house. If you want to kill yourself take that shit down the street," I sighed. I didn't care. I have zero tolerance for dramatics.

Screaming to the top of her lungs now, Chantal yelled, "You're just going to walk away Jullian, like I never existed? You don't care if I take my own life – do you? You selfish Bitch! If I go, you are going with me!"

My eyes got golf ball sized when I saw her remove the gun from her head and point it to the back of Jullian. I yelled, "No!!!!"

POW! POW!

Two shots were fired but Jullian wasn't shot. I saw Chantal hit the ground with two bullet holes to her chest. I turned around and saw Dream holding the smoking gun.

"We don't throw shade, we shoot bullets, right Auntie?" We immediately went into cleanup mode to hide the body.

CHAPTER 4

Nina

Welcome to the missing-persons division. I could have unloaded my entire clip on Chief Raymond for moving me from the homicide division to missing persons after the Banks case. I was persistent in proving that the youngest Banks sister couldn't have killed the victim, due to the trajectory of the bullets. A rookie could have proven that. She had gunpowder on her hands, but four shots were fired. She might have fired the gun, but she didn't fire it at the victim. Darnelle Mitchell was a predominant lawyer. He had looks, power, and money. His family was well-known and highly respected because his father was a district-court judge. The evidence didn't add up. I was pulled off the case when I refused to adhere to the order to close the investigation the day after the murder. It was a murder, but the police department told the media it was self-defense. The politics of it all drove me back to drinking.

"Pour me another stiff one, Ahmad," I said, slamming my fifth shot glass down on the bar counter. Ahmad and his older brother ran Blue. Ahmad was handsome like his brother and a smart kid. He had just graduated from high school with a full scholarship to Duke University. His brother had raised him after the death of his parents. I'd heard he had another brother who had been recently killed by the game. "Ahmad, why does your brother always disappear when I come into the bar? Tell him I won't bite unless he wants me to," I said with a wink. His brother was hella fine, and if he was hiding something, I wanted it to remain hidden. I didn't look for crime. I only responded to it when it called. "I don't know, Detective Ross." He always said the word detective with extra emphasis to remind me that he hadn't forgotten who I was, no matter how cool I seemed to be. "Maybe he's scared of your beauty," he said, wiping down the already-spotless counter with a white towel. Then he leaned over the counter in front of me, showing his waves and fresh cut. He always wore a freshly pressed white T-shirt with fresh jeans, nice sneakers, diamonds in his ears, and a nice diamond watch in the daytime. At night, he would switch to a neatly pressed collared black dress shirt and black slacks with the same accessories. "I don't blame him. If I wasn't a cop, I wouldn't fuck with them either," I said, laughing. He thought it was hilarious as well and was smiling, showing his perfect white teeth. "You have that clean, pretty-boy swag, I see, Ahmad. You got a girlfriend?" I asked. "Nah, I'm too focused on my books, working, and working out. I only have a partial basketball scholarship and a one-year academic scholarship to Duke," he said, grabbing a bottled water to drink. It was getting busy, but thanks to the other bartenders, Malcolm and Akia, we were able to talk for a little bit longer. "They come at me, but after losing my parents, I just don't want to be connected to anyone. It's easier to go on with your future when you're not connected to anyone from your past, Detective," he said with a half-smile.

"Don't let college turn you out," I said, joking.

Laughing, he said, "In college, I will obtain my education to better my future and find my wife to spend it with. Too many men let hoes bring them down, chasing after the pussy. I trust no one, so the one I do decide to trust is going to be my wife. When was the last time you heard a wife selling out a husband who has been good to her? But a hoe—a hoe will roll on you eventually, no matter how good the nigga is. I've seen it happen too many times. It ain't worth it to me," he said with a serious look on his face.

"Damn, Ahmad, I didn't know you were going to go that deep. You almost blew my buzz!" We both started cracking up.

"Here's one on the house. Stay sexy, Detective," he said, and he disappeared into the back. I assumed he was going to change into his signature all-black nightlife outfit. Blue was jumping, as it always was on Friday nights. It had a Philly swag that drew in a lot of Northerners turned Southerners all day every day. In Philly, bars were open and packed all day long. Most of the bars in Charlotte didn't open up until four in the afternoon and didn't get crowded until after seven. However, Blue was the top spot to hit for the African American community. Whether one was old or young, Blue was starting to be the place where everyone went to get away. It had a little bit of everything on the low. At the entrance, to the left was the bar, where they sold the best fish and chicken. There were a couple of booths and round tables to the right, and on the other side was a room with four pool tables. Directly down the middle was a deep red curtain that concealed the dance floor behind it. That was where the crowd headed when they heard their song come on. During the day, the bar played all of the best old-school music, from Otis Redding to Luther Vandross. Between six and seven, karaoke began. After eight, the new-school music started, and after ten on Friday and Saturday nights, the only thing playing was booty-shaking music. That was when the top-of-the-line Atlanta and Charlotte strippers took advantage of the poles. Most of them were college girls from the surrounding cities. North Carolina A&T, Johnson C. Smith, Clark Atlanta, and Spelman were just a few of the historically black colleges that surrounded the Queen City of Charlotte. I graduated from Clark Atlanta and then moved to Charlotte. I had been there ever since.

After my free drink, I grabbed my items and called Seth to tell him to meet me back at my apartment for an all-nighter. He was the first white man I'd ever had. He understood that my heart was unavailable. He also knew we couldn't be together due to a very important reason. He was my Boss. He was my superior, which made fucking him even better. He loved that I was his well-kept secret. I thrived off of his attraction to me. He was 40 but looked as if he was 30 because he was so physically fit. A fine glass of wine, as my mother would say.

"I'm about to assign the Chantal Holmes case right now, but I'm wrapping it up for the night. Believe it or not it's rumored that the last place she was headed to was to see Jullian Banks," Seth said, knowing that news would catch my attention.

"Jullian Banks, huh?" I said, intrigued.

"Yes, Jullian Banks. I figured that would get your attention. Let's talk the case over while I'm licking you over," he said, flirting.

I grabbed my red clutch, took the rest of my drink to the head, and replied, "I'm on my way."

CHAPTER 5

Diamond

I'm a kept bitch right now and I'm loving it. Jay provides me the lifestyle that I am accustomed to and deserves. He is the perfect combination of a Boss and a professional. He has that Idris Elba swag. Funny thing is that I met Jay when I was leaving Boss's grave shortly after he died. He said he was there visiting his brother who was recently murdered. I could see the pain in his eyes which met my pain. He asked me to join him for coffee that afternoon and we have been together ever since. While he is out running his multiple businesses, I'm redecorating our eight-bedroom home. All white everything with a splash of one color – either red, ice blue, yellow, black, or silver - in every room except the living room. The living room is all white except the black and white picture of us hanging over the fireplace. The kitchen is all white, with stainless steel appliances, and a splash of red for the décor. Our room is all white with black and silver accent colors. The patio has all white furniture that surrounds the pool that looks as if it's flowing over into Lake Wylie, which is where we live. It's beautiful and peaceful. My entire closet is all white because that is all that I wear just like Lisa Raye. I may wear colored accessories and shoes, but understand my white never gets dirty unless it is truly necessary. I've been in a few situations where that had to happen. I never planned on killing my brother Sly, Darnelle, or the others, but hell, shit happens. Some things are simply out of your control.

I had so much on my mind due to what had happened to me over my lifetime. I lost my best partners in crime, Boss and West, my best friend, and then my dream of ever having a child with Jay. Jay confessed that he couldn't ever dream of having kids from the very beginning. He said taking care of his brother and sister, who are grown now, was enough. The selfish side of me resented him a little but the mature side of me knew I had to respect it. Since he raised his two siblings, I understood why he felt like he already had kids. To keep myself occupied he suggested that I write as therapy. Who would've thought my writings would have turned into a book. Essence Best seller and number nine on the New York Times list is pretty good for my first book.

I write under the name of Ms. Jones. I chose that name because everyone wants to keep up with the Joneses and everyone wants to keep up with me. It was a perfect fit. I had stories to tell to relieve my stress. Although I'm out of the game, I still feel like someone is watching me like I'm still in it. My girl and I got into too much not to write about it. Damn, I miss my boo. Adrianna had great taste. She is still my best friend in my heart but I will never tell her that – it hurts too much. She and I would have had a great time decorating this place. Jay's baby sister, Jewel, helps me a lot since she lives here with us. She is one of the most humble chicks I know, to be so beautiful. She is the only female that I hang out with because she is the only female that I know who won't try to drop her panties for my man. Since she is Jay's sister I have no choice but to love her because I rock with him.

I am seeing less and less of Jewel lately. I started to ask her if she has a new man but then I thought…I don't really give a fuck. The less I know the less I have to be there to pick up the pieces when she gets hurt. Jewel is still young and wet behind the ears. She hasn't learned that her beauty isn't enough for the streets. Instead of staying in college she dropped out to come live with us. I can't believe Jay even let her do that. He would never let his brother, Ahmad, drop out. Jewel said she is going back next semester. She said that she only needed a semester off. Time will tell. I wouldn't be surprised either way. She is too determined to not finish but she thinks that she has all the time in the world to do it. In my book, I talk about how the world waits for no one. You have to work hard so that you can afford to play harder. Obviously, she didn't read the book yet. If she did then she's stupid for not applying what she read. She was all under me when she first moved in but she is a ghost now. She acts like she doesn't have time for me. I love her but fuck her.

Even though I love Jewel, I don't need her. No one will replace Adrianna anyway. Jewel is just an imitation of my best friend. I haven't spoken to Adrianna since the day I killed Darnelle. I saw her in court when I had to testify but I didn't speak. I decided to let it burn because at the end of the day hoes not loyal. She was sleeping with her sister's man and grilled me for sleeping with hers. What kind of shit is that? The only difference is that I knew I was the mistress but she was in denial about hers.

"Hi baby. You smell good. Is that the new perfume I got you last week?" Jay asked, as he took me into his arms as soon as he came in the house. I was standing in the foyer just admiring how beautiful the house looked. I didn't even hear him come in.

"Yes, baby it is," I said smiling.

Kissing me on my neck he said, "It smells even better on you." This man is really trying to make me fall in love with him. I won't. I mean I can't. I mean I won't and I can't. I could never love him from my heart. My mind says yes so I stay. He is the first man that I can see myself being with for a long time. I want to say forever but forever isn't in my vocabulary.

My father didn't stay forever and my own mother didn't stay forever. Both of them left me and Sly to fend for ourselves. We didn't have a grandmother that was around to take us in. My father's mother was murdered and my mother's mom could care less about us because she could care less than a fuck about herself. That explains why my mother became a crackhead. That's how she met my father. He was her supplier. My father must have fallen in love and decided to get her clean. He moved her out to Harrisburg which is a suburb of Charlotte. The best parks, schools, and best communities are what he wanted for us. My father decided to grow up after my mother gave birth to me and stop selling drugs. They were both twenty seven at the time. He was good with his hands so he started his own home improvement business.

Then Sly was born. One of his first contracts was with New Spirit Church. They invited our family to attend and after three years my father became a deacon. My mother would never fully commit. She was fighting her own demons. My father prayed, prayed, and prayed for her to get saved. It seemed like the more he prayed and went to church the more my mother would go back into the city to hit the pipe. One day my father followed my mother out of the sanctuary during service. He caught my mother buying drugs from a dealer in the back of the church. On another occasion he overheard two men of the church on the church steps discussing how my mother would offer sex for money. He came out from around the corner and whipped the wheels off of both of them. He didn't want to believe it. She lied for weeks. Then, during a counseling session with the Pastor she came out and told the truth. My father was so hurt. Then he became furious when the Pastor admitted that he knew the truth all along because she approached him as well.

That night at home I remember hearing them argue. I put the covers over my head to block them out. Sly was a baby so he slept through it all. My father asked how he could be sure that Sly and I were his children since he was married to a whorish crackhead. He wasn't serious. He just wanted to hurt her feelings to the core like she did him. To my surprise, and to my father's surprise, my mother said, "As a matter of fact, you're right. Neither one of them are yours." My father left the church and us. I never saw him again.

My mother started using at home. She didn't even care that we were home. She could have at least waited until we went to school. She had no respect for us and that's exactly why I have no respect for bitches, especially basic bitches. I never told anyone my story. I started to tell Adrianna but said fuck it. Rule number two is to never show a hoe your weakness even if she is your friend. Why? Because the hoe was a hoe before she was your friend and hoes aren't loyal. That's rule number one: *hoes are not loyal.* I decided to tell Jay tonight over dinner about my childhood. I figured I'd been holding this too long. He needs to know why it's so hard for me to love. He has been so good to me. I may never be able to give him my heart but at least I can give him honesty. I have to tell him before he says those words to me first. I was looking oh so good with my all white fitted low cut Chanel dress on. I couldn't wait to be on Jay's arm. I decided to go downstairs and find him.

I heard him getting dressed when I was in the shower, but that was thirty minutes ago. I know he is ready to go by now. Walking down the steps I saw Ms. Valeria the maid. She was standing by the front door smiling at me. "Ms. Val, have you seen Jay?"

"He is that way Madame," she said, pointing with a smile.

"Ms. Val, you don't have to call my Madame, just call me Diamond. That's the shit they say in the movies and we are not in the movies." We both started laughing but I knew she would still call me Madame. She is just professional like that. She loves us. We consider her family. She reminds me of the mother I should have had. I think she sees me as a daughter too but she senses that I can't open my heart up to her. She also senses that I don't have a mother because if I did I would have mentioned her by now. The way she looks at me tells me that she can see straight through me sometimes.

As I started walking, I started to see rose petals. "Baby this is beautiful!" Jay had red rose petals leading down the white hardwood floors out to the back patio. I followed them and there he was sipping on some wine with a black tuxedo on.

"Anything for you baby," he said with a smile. He had the staff prepare a dinner for us on the patio. I saw the Jacuzzi steaming with lit white candles surrounding the edges. Usher was playing and my heart was pounding. I have to stop myself from falling in love with this man. We danced, laughed, ate, and sipped wine for hours. By the end of the night he and I were in the Jacuzzi doing everything you could imagine. After that last orgasm I almost told him that I loved him.

Instead, I called his name and that made him cum sooner than he wanted too. "Come on baby let me dry you off and take you to bed. We have to get up early in the morning."

"For what?" I asked.

"I want us, for the first time, to go to church tomorrow. I just want to live life differently," he said from his heart. My heart stopped.

"Church? Baby, I don't know if I can do that." He looked at me strangely while drying me off and asked me why. So, I decided to tell him my story. I didn't tell him that is the reason that I trust and love no one but I told him the story. I even told him how my mother died.

"Word Ma! Damn, that had to be heavy. I wish you would have told me sooner," he said, kissing me softly with his full brown lips on my forehead.

CHAPTER 6

Nina

"Good morning beautiful," is what I heard when I answered my phone while driving.

"Cut the crap Malcolm. Why were you at Blue the other night? I didn't want to draw attention to you, so I acted like I didn't know you, of course." I said, trying to get to the point. Detective Malcolm was too sexy and would be the perfect guy for me if his job did not require him to go deep undercover for long periods of time. He worked in my former department, Homicide.

"According to your new caseload, I conveniently had assigned to you, we will be spending a lot more time together," he said in a flirtatious tone.

"What rabbit did you pull out your hat? Speak fast because I'm on my way to…" He cut me off.

"…to your mom's. I know, because for weeks you left my bed every Sunday morning and went to your mom's until one day you decided not to come back. We are not going to finally talk about that today or are we?" I got quiet. Then my eyes grew big when I saw his undercover Benz parked outside of my mother's home when I came around the corner. He opened the door to let me out by the hand. I couldn't help but blush. He knew I wanted him but he also knew I was running from him.

We were face to face now and the chemistry was everything. My God he smelled so good. He handed me some files. "There better be a good reason for this pop up visit," I said twirling my hair gazing into his eyes. He had me with this face to face visit. He knew I could only be strong over the phone. The truth is I don't know how to use my heart because I purposely haven't used it in so long. Homicide took everything out of me. He was staring back at me with stars in his eyes. He gently grabbed me by the chin and kissed me softly on the lips.

"Trust me, there is. You will be hearing from me soon," he said, as he jumped back in his car and pulled off. After realizing that I wasn't breathing I quickly reviewed the files. To my pleasant surprise, they were the missing person files of Sly Jones and Lady Hartwell. I couldn't help but smile because Malcolm knew I wanted to nail the Banks sisters for the cover up. We suspected that the murders surrounding the Banks family and the missing persons, directly after the deaths, are all tied together somehow. We haven't figured it out yet but we will. Since I can't catch them by knocking on the front door I'm going to have to go around back and kick in the back door.

I always stopped by my parents' house every Sunday morning for breakfast. It was perfect timing because I knew my father wouldn't be there. Every Sunday he went to play golf at the country club. It would be late afternoon before he would return. My mom would have breakfast ready at exactly ten o'clock a.m., because she knew that I wouldn't be late. I'm never late, so she made sure that my plate was placed on the table at ten o'clock on the dot. The smell of crisp turkey bacon, scrambled eggs with cheese, and blueberry muffins made me smile every time I walked into the house. The house has looked the same since I was a little girl. My mother did the same thing every day. She went walking every day during the week at nine in the morning with our dog Bentley. When she returned she would shower, dress, and be out the door by eleven to make it to her massage session with Andre at Diva Salon and Spa. Friday was an exception. On Fridays she would get her hair and nails done. Saturdays used to be date night for her and my dad but he always claims he is too tired, now she goes shopping from sunup to sundown. On Sundays she cooks breakfast for me and makes it to church by eleven thirty in the morning for service. I used to go to church with her sometimes but there were rumors that the Pastor is gay. I'm not the one to believe in rumors but after careful observation of his mannerisms I started to believe them. No real man stands with his hands on his hips like a woman, waves goodbye like a girl, nor says, "hoooooney" when having a conversation. Still, you couldn't tell my mother nothing about her Pastor. Pastor Leon was the greatest man next to God and Jesus in her eyes. I noticed that my father stopped going, too, about a year ago, when the rumors surfaced. I don't really talk to my father much so I've never asked him why. If you are not talking about achievements or investments he didn't have much to say to you. I used to be able to discuss anything with my father until I became a cop. He acted as if being a cop was the lowest of the low. I wish I could talk to him about my boyfriends, my cases, or everyday issues. I tried to have conversations with him but he would always cut me short if I spoke about anything other than success so I stopped trying.

"Mama, what happened to the blueberry muffins? Strawberry is good but you always make blueberry muffins. Let me find out you're changing the game up on me." I said, laughing, but secretly wondering what was going on with her. I was getting ready to move the yellow envelope over, away from my plate, so that I wouldn't get anything on it but before I had a chance to move it, Mama snatched it out of my hands. "Jesus! Are there crime scene photos that will incriminate your or something in there?" I said, playfully.

"You will never find evidence on me because whatever I chose to do no one will ever catch me," she said. I don't think she was joking. Something wasn't right. She wasn't wearing her Sunday morning outfit. Normally, when I come over she has on her silk red slip and housecoat set, which she always put on after her shower. She always had an updo hairstyle already done, church music playing, with her church clothes laid out. She was a young looking fifty-three year old. When we were out everyone thought that she was my older sister but never my mother.

This Sunday, she had on the pajamas she slept in with her brown hair hanging just above her shoulders. She reminds me of a younger version of Toni Braxton's mother, which is ironic because everyone says I look like Toni Braxton's sister, Trina Braxton. People mistake me for her all the time. I love it because she is beautiful! I could see my mother pouring orange juice into a glass from the family room. I turned the music up when I heard that the next song was a Shirley Caesar song because I knew that my mother would tell me to turn it up. Shirley Caesar is her favorite gospel singer.

"Baby breakfast is ready," she said with a happy tone. I walked into the library to see if my graduate degree was still on the wall. I figured my father might just take it down after a year of us not saying more than hello and bye. I ran my fingers across the top of the fireplace where all of my awards sat. "Young lady did you hear me say breakfast is ready?" She said in a snappy tone.

"Yes ma'am, I did. I'm sorry. I'm coming right now." I said, quickly, before she came after me. Even though I'm strapped and work with criminals every day, I'm still afraid of my mother. Every child should be scared of their parents even when they are grown. If they are not, then something is wrong. I always felt that if I didn't come after the second time she called me that she would be right behind me in less than two point two seconds with a switch in her hand. I know I'm grown now but that is still my mama.

Nina Samone Ross, Summa Cum Laude, was written on my college degree, which hung proudly on the wall. I told my parents that they could have it since they seemed to be more proud of it than they are of me. Since my father is a judge, and I showed great interest in law, everyone thought that I would become a lawyer or a judge. I always knew that I just wanted to be a homicide detective. Now that I've been moved to Missing Persons everybody is on my *fuck you list* especially my father. I sat down in the breakfast sunroom waiting for my mother to say the grace. To my surprise she just started eating. I looked at her, and then she looked at me with a mouth full of food. "Are you going to say grace?" I asked.

"I already did when I called you the first time." She said, being funny. For some reason I didn't believe her this time. She stood up, went down to the basement from the kitchen, and came back up with a bottle of wine. "You want some baby?" She asked, popping the cork. I had to ask myself if I was dreaming.

"Of course, pour me a glass." I didn't know what had gotten into my mother but change is good. We sat there all morning drinking wine, having girl talk, and laughing about everything under the sun. We moved the party into the formal living room which was odd. The living room was all white and gold. The room was just for show. No one ever sat in this room but for some reason, with our red wine, we had our feet kicked up on the furniture like we were in the family room. I fell asleep. I woke up three hours later to my father walking into the room.

CHAPTER 7

Adrianna

"Welcome to DivaStar," I said, without looking in the customer's direction, who I'd just heard walk in. I was too busy trying not to fall off the ladder while turning the channel on the flat screen to the music station, since no one could find the stupid remote. I sure miss my sister Jullian helping out in the store. It was starting to piss me off looking for the remote every day. I should've just demanded that it stay on gospel all day. Hell, we needed Jesus up in there with all of our spirits. Sometimes the store got boring but it was less stress than being in the game. Although, I did miss the rush! I especially missed Diamond. I had no business climbing a ladder in my fitted royal blue BeBe dress anyway. I started laughing to myself, missed a step, and slipped. Luckily, I was caught by the most handsome man that I'd ever seen in my life. Smelling so good, clean cut with the prettiest smile and brown skin he said, "The moment I saw you Ma I knew that I would never let you fall." The way he said it had so much meaning behind it. Our eyes were transfixed on each other's for what seemed like minutes. Then my sister Jullian walked into the store smiling from ear to ear when she saw the sexiness holding me.

"What do we have here?" Jullian said, clearing her throat.

The handsome man placed me down and said, "I don't know but I would like to."

I tried to play it cool and acted like what just happened didn't happen. "What can I help you with today in the store?" I asked, as I walked over to the counter. Jullian was mean-mugging me, telling me with her facial expression that I'm fucking up. He walked over towards me but to my surprise walked right past me over to a pair of shoes behind me. Of course he would eye the most expensive shoes in the store. I'd started to like this man more and more.

"I would like to have those in a size 8 please". When he pointed to the shoes I saw his Hublot Big Bang Ferrari Titanium watch on his wrist. The diamonds were blinding me. It was the only piece of jewelry that he had on because he needed nothing else. Immediately I knew I wasn't dealing with an average nigga. I saw Jullian peep and start admiring the watch as well. Those watches with the diamonds can cost millions.

Trying not to stare I said, "These just came in today. Twenty-two hundred but for you I will give you twenty percent off," I said with a flirty smile. Jullian rolled her eyes because she knew after I saw the watch I was all in. She knew it would take more than a fine man that smelled good to hold my attention. Only money could do that. Fine men come a dime a dozen but fine and rich doesn't. Now that he had my attention all I had to do was walk to the cash register with my signature walk and he would be mine.

I grabbed the shoes as Jullian flipped the closed sign on. We were closing up early to join the festivities of the CIAA in uptown Charlotte. We both said we needed drinks after the drama that took place earlier at Charisma's house with Chantal. Mr. Handsome was our last client and

I'm so glad that I was there when he came. I'd felt him staring at me from the back. Jullian was still waiting by the door where she first came in. I could tell she wanted to give us some space just in case he wanted to ask me out. What man wouldn't? I hit my signature walk and rung him up. He flashed his perfect smile and said, "It was nice meeting you." I was thinking to myself, *okay now hurry up and ask me for my number.* Then he turned around and headed towards the door. My mouth dropped wide open. I'd hinted to Jullian to intervene or do something. She just looked at me with the *bitch you stupid* look and *no I'm not helping you* look on her face. I'd felt so stupid. My signature walk always worked. Was I losing my swag? Should I have stopped him? I wanted to, but hell no. I'm Adrianna Banks.

What the fuck do I look like chasing after a nigga? If he'd wanted it he could've gotten it but I was damn sure not about to just offer it. I waved my hand in my pride like *just let him go* and turned my back before the door even closed behind him. Then, I went to the back to cut all the lights off. After I heard the doorbell *ding dong* as he exited out of the door I had a woosah moment. Jullian rushed over to me as I was coming back out from the back.

"You think I'm going to say something, but guess what? I'm not. I'm not because there is no reason to say anything because you already know what's going to be said."

"Jullian, shut up hoe and come on," I said laughing. "Where are we going tonight? I'm so ready for a drink after this."

"It's CIAA weekend and we are finally going to Blue. I heard tonight is the night for the grown and sexy," Jullian said, admiring her pretty face in the shop window. I locked up and we were one way to Blue.

We got to Blue and it was everything that everyone said it was. We immediately went to the bar to get a drink and to our surprise we already knew the bartender. *I wouldn't picture him working here;* Jullian's face said when she looked at me. He just nodded, as to say what's up and gave us both Apple Martinis all night without saying a word. We understood the drinks were on the house. *I sure miss Charisma*, I'd thought to myself. She needed to get out the house more but on that night she needed to be home with Dream; however, not for Dream, but for herself.

Dream was not as shook as we expected her to be after killing Chantal. Charisma was the one that we needed to calm down after she saw blood everywhere. She tried to run over to Chantal to help her. Jullian and I both already knew she was DOA. We both had to run and grab Charisma. We didn't want her adding more evidence to the crime scene with DNA and etc. We needed to get that body out of there. To make things even worse a white Charger with black tint started to come up to the house. Everybody got so quiet that you could've heard a leaf fall from a tree and hit the ground. The door opened and I saw a young hustler step out wearing fresh wheat Timberlands, black pants, a navy NY Yankee fitted hat, and a fresh white Tee. His eyewear was Cartier and the bling and cut of the diamonds in his ear told me this wasn't just some ordinary dude. He immediately assessed the situation. I grabbed my gun from Dream but when I turned to point it at him I wasn't surprised he had one pointed right at me.

He sensed the tension but instead of buckling under pressure he asked, "Anything I can help you ladies with?" He looked in the car again and saw exactly what we were knee deep in. Then I heard Dream say, "Yes" at the same time Jullian and I said, "Hell No!"

"Who the fuck is this, Dream?" I said, looking him directly in the eyes. He and I both quickly comprehended that we were somehow from the same worlds and that either one of us would shoot if necessary. My ears heard him offer to help us but I'm not too quick to let anyone in.

Dream interrupted us by saying "This is the guy I was telling you about earlier, whose girl has a problem with me."

He quickly denounced what Dream said by stating, "That's not my girl."

"This is Ahmad. Ahmad, meet my aunties, my mom, and the Banks sisters," she said with a grin, because she knew this was a crazy way for all of us to meet.

He withdrew his gun and offered me his hand like a gentleman. Then he said, "I'm in this with you now so what would you like for me to do?" Jullian gave me the signal to chill.

I withdrew my nine and said, "Whew! I need a drink."

"An Apple Martini would be perfect for us right now" Jullian said. We all began to laugh except Charisma. Charisma was still in a place of shock but she knew we had to move and move quickly.

I'd wanted to call my old clean-up crew but no one could know where my family lived anymore. I'd been out the game for a minute now so they didn't have a reason to be loyal to me. I couldn't take the chance of Charisma losing her entire career or the chance of Dream going to jail. After explaining all of this, we all knew that we had to do the clean-up job ourselves. We placed the body in Chantal's trunk. When we got to our final destination Jullian could tell by my face that I was still contemplating killing Ahmad. I mean...who leaves witnesses behind? Then again, he proved to be instrumental. He acted like he had buried bodies before by the way he moved without waiting for orders on how to handle the body and how he positioned Chantal's car to go into the lake. We drove it to an isolated part of the lake at Lake Norman, and watched it sink down to where the rest of the bodies that Boss, West, Diamond, and I had laid to rest there. The more the water began to submerge the beautiful car the more we were relieved that it was almost over. Well, at least Jullian and I were. Out of sight, out of mind for us; yet, Charisma would need a little bit longer to get over this. The good thing is that we could count on her doing it for her daughter and at the end of the day she was a Banks. Aside from that - nothing else needs to be said.

We danced to every song that came on for the first hour and a half. Jullian had on a short, emerald green dress. Against her light skin, the dress made her green eyes pop. The bitch was bad but never flaunted it. I always forget that she is *licky, licky* with chicks, until I see a chick checking her out or I see her checking one out. "I see you checking her out. Bitch no kisses on the lips for Thanksgiving or Christmas." We fell out laughing.

Still dancing and checking back to see if the girl was watching, she asked, "What's the difference between dick in my mouth and pussy in my mouth?"

"Bitch I sucked dick but I be damned if I'll lick pussy. Secondhand licking might just kill you." We were so tipsy that we were cracking up at everything the other one said. Drinks were coming for us all night on somebody's tab. It was probably some lame who was too shy to approach us. That was his loss. I didn't ask and I didn't care. Jullian didn't seem to care either because she didn't ask.

Jullian must have been reading my mind. "I miss Charisma too sis. Give her a few more months to get adjusted and then it's on and popping again." I was about to take a break from the floor but all of a sudden the music changed up to *Love in the Club* by Beyoncé featuring Young Jeezy and Usher. That used to be my jam. Jullian looked at me with a smirk on her face as if she requested the song to come on just for me or something. I felt someone gently grab my hand. I turned to mean mug whoever it was but it was Mr. Handsome. My face lit up like a Christmas tree. I didn't have time to fake it. He could see that I was melting and obviously, so was he.

"May I have this dance Slim?" he asked, but never waited for an answer. He walked me to the middle of the dance floor and started making love to me with our clothes on. He was rich, handsome, smelled good, and then I found out he could dance. I thought I was going to faint. "I'm glad you came. I see your sister did exactly what I wanted her to do. I slid my business card to her as I was walking out of your store today, indicating I wanted her to bring you here. I'm the owner," he whispered in my ear. I scanned the crowd and saw Jullian talking to the woman who was checking her out earlier. The woman seemed so familiar as if I had seen her on TV. She had dark hair, dark eyes, and a cute magazine model shape. Her image didn't fit the scene. She seemed like she would be in the back of a private club rubbing elbows with the Bosses. She looked very comfortable and powerful at her private table eyeing Jullian. The man standing on the wall beside her booth looked like he could be her bodyguard. The beautiful lady summoned for Jullian to come over to her table by patting the seat beside her while looking directly at Jullian. When Jullian looked back at me I gave her the biggest smile to thank her. He stepped back to get a full view of me and said, "My name is Jackson and you are?"

"My name is Adrianna. Adrianna Banks."

"Adrianna, you are beautiful." The chemistry between us was undeniable. He smelled so damn good. His swag was impeccable. I could have eaten him up. He had put it on me on the dance floor. Towards the end when he came up from freaking me, he kissed me. It was so passionate and so spontaneous that I couldn't resist kissing him back. Who was this man who had just taken my breath away? How dare he kiss me on our first date! Hell this wasn't even our first date. I'd just met him but it seemed as if I'd known him for years. I had never felt like this before. Boss didn't even get a kiss until two months later. I felt myself about to cum and I had to pull back. I hadn't had sex in months. I had to ask myself was it us or was it the fact that I hadn't had any in a while. Who was I fooling? I'd been around long enough to know that it was us. This chemistry was truly undeniable. I still didn't know who he bought those shoes for. They sure weren't for him. I was going to ask him later because at that time, I was enjoying the moment. He took me into the coat check area which was dark and unused that night. He pulled the black curtains to help hide us behind the counter, lifted one of my legs up over his arm, and then slid into me. It was the closest thing to heaven because I was surely on cloud nine. I asked myself while smelling his Creed cologne, *what in the hell did I just fall into?*

CHAPTER 8

Diamond

"Hi Stranger," I said to Jewel as she pulled up to the front of the house right behind me in her black-on-black Porsche.

"Why does your man have to hog the five car garage," she said, slamming the door catching the bottom of her dress in it.

"Jewel, what the hell is wrong with you? You better not let Jay see you like this. Why didn't you call your new boo thing to drive you home?"

She said staggering, "I didn't want to bother him. It's late." I rolled my eyes in disgust.

"Baby girl if you can't call the man you are fucking in an event of an emergency then he isn't your man and more importantly you shouldn't be fucking him."

She looked right at me trying to be serious and said, "You will meet him sooner than you think. Real soon." She started to laugh uncontrollably as if it were the funniest thing she'd ever said. I shook my head thinking, this young, pretty girl has so much to learn. I couldn't help but laugh at the way she was walking up the steps to the front door.

"If Ms. Val sees you like this you are going to get it. You look white girl wasted. Just come on before Jay gets home," I said, laughing at her trying to go through her purse looking for her keys. This bitch was so wasted that she didn't even realize the car was still running with the lights on. I just leaned against my truck waiting for her to realize it.

I thought about helping her, but I passed. I was wearing all white, as usual, dipped in the new diamonds. Jay and I had gone out earlier and purchased our outfits for that day and the next day, down to the shoes and accessories. I had dipped off for a few to find him a gift for his birthday that was coming up soon. I was fly and I didn't feel like being thrown up on. Ahmad called Jay when we were leaving our last party of the weekend. He wanted Jay to come by Blue so I went home solo. We had the best time in Uptown Charlotte celebrating the CIAA. It wasn't even planned. He met me uptown for business and our day turned into pleasure. The day parties were the best. That was when the Grown and Sexy came out to play. I had a book signing the next day at the Convention Center. I wanted to go by to see the setup. It was so turned up in Uptown that Jay and I decided to go crash the Epicentre. We went to a few day parties and had the best time. My baby sure can dance. The way he holds me on the dance floor makes me forget where I am. The vender told me that they had to switch my area to a larger area because they expected it to be a larger turnout than originally expected.

I was on a natural high at the time and Jewel was not going to spoil it.

Still struggling, looking in her purse she said desperately, "I know I had my keys Diamond. If I didn't I wouldn't be able to get home. This is really pissing me off. I mean how hard can it be to lose your keys in a clutch purse, Diamond? Diamond......Diamond?" When she realized that I wasn't responding she turned around to look at me. Then I looked at her Porsche still running with the lights on. When she realized the car was still running, we both fell out laughing.

"Girl, I really need you to get your life, Jewel," I said helping her up the stairs and past Ms. Val's room. When we opened Jewel's bedroom door the light came on. It was Ms. Val standing there with two aspirin and a glass of water for Jewel. I helped Ms. Val help Jewel get showered and ready for bed. I told Ms. Val to go to bed and I would watch Jewel all night. I thought, *What if she threw up?* Don't judge me. I cared. I just didn't care too much. You saw what happened the last time I cared about someone.

"Baby, let's go to bed," Jay said, pulling me up. I'd fallen asleep sitting in the chair beside Jewel's bed with my head on her bed. "Thank you so much for taking care of my sister. Clearly, she had a hard night. Our brother said she was at Blue. The real reason he called me was to tell me that she was fucked up and that he needed me to take her home. He couldn't leave because he was running the club and you know he couldn't trust no niggas to do it. I tried to be in and out but there was a V.I.P. guest there that I had to attend to for at least a few minutes. As you see, I wasn't there long. Diamond, I didn't tell you because I didn't want to ruin your night. We had a perfect day, didn't we bae?" he said, with love in his eyes, as he took off my new heels that I still had on.

"How did you know that she was here Jay?" I asked pulling him in between my legs so that we could make love.

"Ms. Val called me and told me that you two were outside so I came home." Then he kissed my ear and whispered softly, "By the way I turned your truck off Ma because you left it running out front."

The local artists who were booked for the book signing were wonderful. Jay came but left early stating that he had a business emergency. However, to my surprise, Jay booked my favorite poet, Lyric, who gave a spoken word between the signing and the discussion segment. The discussion segment was over and surprisingly Jewel had not arrived yet to assist me with collecting the money for my sales. Jewel had one job and couldn't even do that. *Sigh, What happened to you? The event is over now,* I texted. I heard my phone buzz back with her reply but before I could check it I noticed I was eye to eye with Adrianna Banks.

CHAPTER 9

Adrianna

Jullian was steaming hot at me for arriving late to pick her up for The Ms. Jones book signing for *These Hoes Be Winning*. I don't even have to read the book because Jullian has talked my head off about everything in it. I must admit that the parts she read to me had been very good. You can tell the writer was either a Boss chick or personally knew a Boss chick. We arrived at the venue and I was surprised that there were hundreds of people there to meet the author. Since Jullian was still mad at me she walked ahead of me to go sit down. She didn't even see what happened next. Before entering the main room from the lobby, someone pulled me into a side office. Flashbacks from the kidnapping flooded me. I went for the blade in my silk ponytail. As I lifted my hand to grab it he forced my arms above my head and against the back of the door, then he kissed me. I immediately knew by the passionate kiss that it was Jackson.

"What are you doing here?" I asked between kisses.

"My sister wanted an autographed book. She was the woman I was buying the shoes for from your store. You look so sexy in this red dress," he said kissing me on my neck. I had on my favorite red maxi dress. It hugged my curves just right. I was in a euphoric state of mind. This man smelled and looked amazing, and his kisses felt so good.

As I began to get wet I lightly pushed him off and said with lust in my eyes, "You have not earned me yet. I don't even know you yet."

He replied, "You have not earned me yet either. I don't even know you yet." He then started to unzip his navy blue dress pants, while lifting up one of my legs, and started grinding his manhood against my bare vajayjay. I lost all sense of direction. I knew then it was getting ready to go down heavy. "You want it slow or fast?" he asked with a confident sexy whisper in my ear.

"Slowww Daddy," I said as I began to leak. He felt my wetness and entered. He slow grinded me on the back of the door until we both exploded. We promised to meet up later tonight for round two. We kissed goodbye as I left out of the office first to go find Jullian in the main room.

"Where did you go and why are you glowing? Jullian asked, suspiciously. I told her what just happened. She was so shocked that she forgot that she was mad at me for being late. The author's area was surrounded by fans that we couldn't even see her. Checking myself out in the mirror to make sure I still looked flawless after my impromptu sexcapade, I asked, "Whatever happened to that beautiful lady you were talking to at Blue the other night? She was most definitely a Boss." Jullian was too excited that the crowd was finally going back to their seats so that we could get a view of the author that she didn't even look at me when she replied firmly.

"When I found out what she wanted I told her the same thing I keep telling you. I am not gay."

I made a mental note not to ever joke with her about her sexuality again because clearly she is no longer laughing. I was already late for the book signing. I didn't need my sister mad at me again. The host asked everyone to take their seats for the discussion. "Did you get your book signed already?" I asked.

"I will afterwards. Then the line won't be as long." Jullian said as she checked to see who was calling her. Then I heard my phone go off. "It's just Charisma. You've already had too many distractions today Adrianna so place your phone on silent," she demanded. I felt that she was right so I did.

When we saw Diamond come out we were floored! The discussion was great. I started to grab the mic and ask a question just to be funny. Then I remembered who I was dealing with and changed my mind. I decided to leave. "No you can't leave now. We just sat down. If you stand up now she might notice you." Jullian said out of concern. She knew how Diamond and I felt for one another and secretly prayed that we reconciled.

"As soon as everyone stands up Jullian I am out of here" I said in frustration, crossing my arms and legs, showing my discontentment.

When it was over Jullian begged me to stay while she got her book autographed. "Most people got their book autographed before the discussion so it shouldn't take long." Jullian said trying to convince me to stay. The line moved quicker than I thought but I was still ready to go...immediately! I watched her get closer and closer to Diamond. She knew better than to tell Diamond that I was here. Killing time I looked down on my phone to check my messages and I saw seven missed calls from Charisma so I returned her call.

I ran over to Jullian who had just made it to Diamond's table. Diamond looked like she saw a ghost when she saw me. We had so much mixed emotions in our eyes, staring at each other but she could tell I was in a crisis. "Jullian we have to go. Charisma just called and said Daddy was rushed to the hospital and it's not looking good," I sadly said, grabbing her by the arm to leave. As Jullian was driving to the hospital, I texted Jackson telling him that I have to cancel our plans for tonight. He texted me back but I didn't have a chance to read his response. We finally got to Daddy's room. Mama, Aunt Diane, Charisma, Rashad, Dream, and shockingly, Kendra, were all there.

Jullian asked, "Where is he? Did they take Daddy for testing?"

The doctor walked in and silence filled the room. "I'm sorry. There was nothing more that we could do," he said softly.

"Oh my God, his liver finally failed," Jullian said. Charisma and I looked at her like what do you mean 'finally failed'?

"You knew and didn't tell us!" Charisma screamed. She walked over to Jullian as if she was going to hit her but Mama stepped in front of her.

Just above a whisper Aunt Diane stated, "Your father requested that she kept his confidence."

"His confidence?! I'm the oldest! " Charisma said still screaming and trying to get around Mama to come for Jullian's neck. The Doctor ran out the room to get security. Jullian started pointing her finger towards Charisma over Kendra's head, who was now trying to hold Jullian back from getting in Charisma's face.

"Bitch you better fall back before I knock you back. You might be the oldest but I will drag you in this mutherfucking hospital! You're not shit without your badge, Ms. Probation Officer! You might know how to shoot better than me, but you can't throw hands better than me. Right now, I am not what you want!"

Charisma lost it then and said, "That's why I can't trust you Bitches! You Hoes are not loyal! No disrespect to your sister, Kendra, but Jullian you let Daddy's girlfriend, Chantal, eat your pussy while he was in the house!" Rashad grabbed Charisma and tried to pull her out of the room like a good husband but before he got her completely out she slid one more verbal assault out of her mouth. "And Adrianna, you know you're the family Hoe! We can't trust you either! Did you really think Darnelle was going to run off into the sunset with you? Both of you hoes went from main chicks to side chicks. Once a man promotes the side chick to the main chick, guess what position becomes available?" I went to punch her in her face and that's when Diamond showed up with flowers in the doorway. She dropped the flowers to grab my arm as I swung on Charisma. Thanks to Diamond I couldn't get to that ass, but Jullian did. Jullian slid under the radar when Charisma was throwing shots at me and punched Charisma right in the eye. I saw Jullian getting ready to hit Charisma too and deep inside it gave me real satisfaction. We made such a scene at the hospital that we all were asked to leave immediately if we couldn't calm down.

Mama began to let out a cry that can only be heard when someone has just lost the love of their life. In that moment everyone else began to feel Daddy's loss and began to cry also. Everyone... except Diamond and myself. We just weren't built like that. Everyone else was sad but I wanted to kill somebody. Maybe it was just the Scorpio in me.

CHAPTER 10

Jullian

I felt bad for hitting my sister but in that moment she deserved it. She has no idea the burden I had to carry keeping that secret for Daddy. We kept it to protect them. Adrianna and Charisma were going through so much at the time that we didn't want to add more stress. After the atmosphere calmed down Mom filled everyone in on why Daddy didn't want anyone to know. After mom shared that information, it made everyone feel better. Kendra told us that she had to file a missing person's report on Chantal. She said she stopped by Dad's house to ask him if he had heard from Chantal and that's when she found him, in his car, in front of the house, slumped over. I guess he was trying to drive himself to the hospital. Dream arrived and Rashad took her down to the lobby to tell her that her grandfather had just passed away. While he was doing that, I noticed Diamond showing Adrianna a text she had just received. Their entire demeanor changed and they were speaking to each other through their eyes. Diamond broke their stare. As she went over to hug Mama she said, "My condolences to your family. If you need anything I'm still just one call away." She gave mama her author business card with her number on it. Then she left the room so fast, I felt like in a blink she was gone. Mama was grieving too much to even notice that she was the author of the book Jullian kept telling everyone about.

Adrianna asked me to walk down the hall with her. As soon as we closed my father's hospital room door she grabbed my hand and pleaded, "Jullian, you have to cover for me and tell mama I got so sick I had to leave. If I tell her she will know that I'm lying."

Complexed, I asked, "Where are you going? Does this have to do with Diamond's text?"

With a sigh she said, "Yes. Just cover for me. You know I wouldn't leave the family at this time if it wasn't super important, right? Right? Diamond left to go get her car. I have to meet her downstairs in five minutes. Thank you sis. I got to go."

I went to the ladies restroom down the hall. I just needed some time alone. I leaned on the sink with my head down with my heart in pieces. I betrayed my father. I betrayed myself. "I can't believe I let Chantal turn me out," I said aloud staring at my reflection in the mirror. The toilet flushed in one of the stalls and my heart stopped. I thought to myself, *Oh my God someone heard me.* Then I remembered – no one would be at the hospital besides family that would even know who Chantal was and the family, along with Kendra, was still in Daddy's room.

A pretty lady exited the stall and walked over next to me to wash her hands. After glancing at me in the mirror, she said, "No matter how much we prepare, we can never prepare enough for heartbreak." I smiled and shook my head in agreement. Then she turned to me to look directly in my eyes and asked, "Are you here to see family or a friend?" She wore no makeup because her natural beauty was flawless. She was simple but very attractive. *Not my type*, I thought. I mean I don't have a type regarding women because I'm not gay. I just had a gay experience. I don't know why I felt the need to answer her. She just had that presence that commanded respect.

"I'm here for family. My father just passed," I said, drying my hands under the dryer. The heat felt so good. I thought I would cry in the restroom but I didn't.

She stopped applying her lip gloss, turned to look at me with sorrow and said, "I'm very sorry for your loss. I can completely understand it because I just lost my parents too." Then she went back to applying her lip gloss in the mirror but still looking directly at me via my reflection. "I'm sure you and Chantal will work things out. Looks like you might need a hug from her. When was the last time you saw her?"

I could hear Dream screaming down the hallway at the same time a knock came on the ladies restroom door. I knew then that Rashad had just told Dream. The lady could tell that I recognized that scream by the look on my face. "I'm sorry. I have to go check on my niece. It was nice meeting you." When I opened the restroom door, to my amazement, Jackson was standing there holding a perfect dozen of white roses. "Hey

Jackson! What are you doing here?" I asked with a confused and shocked look on my face. Seeing him holding flowers was a tad awkward but sexy because he had this gangster professional swag that you just had to be born with. They don't make them like him anymore. Most men now don't already come assembled. Before he could answer, the lady in the restroom had to slide by me to leave because I was, rudely, still standing in the doorway awaiting an answer from Jackson.

As he was looking at the lady sliding past me, strangely, he replied, "Your sister texted me on the way to the hospital to tell me your dad was here. I wanted to show my support and bring her some flowers."

I couldn't help but wonder why he had looked at me and the lady so strangely. I had hoped Adrianna didn't tell him that I was a lesbian because I'm not. I'm not gay!

"Nice flowers," the lady said with a grin to Jackson. Then she walked away. Funny thing is that I felt that I would see her again.

"Adrianna just left. Give the flowers to our mother instead." I said, pointing to the room two doors down. He and I both knew that would make a great impression on Adrianna if he did.

He wasn't nervous at all. His confidence made him more attractive as if he needed any help. Adrianna loved confidence in a man almost as much as she loved money. "I have to go check on my niece down the hall the other way but thank you so much for coming by." I wasn't ready to tell anyone not alone a stranger that Daddy didn't make it. I was still processing the loss myself. He would catch on when he went to the room. He gave me a warm hug. Lord Jesus that man smelled good. Then he went to give my mother the roses for Adrianna.

As I was walking towards the seventh floor lobby, where Dream and Rashad were, Kendra was coming out of the hospital room. Due to the scream, Kendra was going to check up on Dream. She immediately turned to her right, towards the scream. I was to her left, so she didn't see me. I stopped to text Adrianna that Jackson came to show support and was about to meet the family. I was hoping that would put a little smile on her face. When I looked up, after texting, I saw Kendra down the hallway leaning against the wall as if she were listening to Dream and Rashad's conversation. As I was walking up behind her to curse her nosey ass out I heard Dream say between sobbing, "And that's why we killed Chantal, Daddy. We had no choice. Now, God is punishing us with grandpa's early death."

Kendra's body became stiff in shock and my eyes grew as big as moth balls. Something had to be done and quick. I asked myself, *what would Adrianna do?* I saw a hospital cart full of fresh linens. I noticed an empty room across from where we were standing outside of the small lobby. I looked in front and behind me and saw no one standing in the hallway. I quickly snatched a pillow case off the linen cart, put it over Kendra's head so tight and quick that she didn't even have a chance to react, dragged her into the empty hospital room, and kicked the door closed with my foot.

After about what seemed like an eternity of suffocating her, I took her shirt off, put a hospital gown on her, and then placed her body on the hospital bed as if she was a patient. *Buzz!* It was Adrianna calling me. I was so happy to see Adrianna's face on my caller ID that I didn't know what to do. The bad part is, seeing her face on my iPhone screen made me snap out of role-playing that I was Adrianna. *I'm not this ruthless or am I?* I'd told myself again that this was a one-time

situation just like my situation with Chantal. I'm
not a murderer nor am I gay. I am not gay!

"Adrianna! Oh My God! I just had to kill
Kendra!" I said in a panic.

"Kendra!" Adrianna and Diamond both said
over Diamond's car speakerphone. Adrianna had
her phone hooked up to Diamond's car Bluetooth.

"Wait….What?" Diamond asked in complete
surprise.

"She found out didn't she?" Adrianna asked,
already knowing the answer. "No time to feel
bad. You had to do what you had to do. At this
point I need you to bring to body to the lake. We
will be waiting but hurry up." I could feel the
hairs standing up on my arms.

"Bring the body? I'm not moving a dead body.
You need to come back here Adrianna. You sound
crazy as - ." She cut me off.

"Look Bitch, get a hold of yourself. As bad as
I want to come back I can't. We are on another
mission that has us on the clock. All you have to
do is get the body to your trunk and bring it here.
We will take care of the rest. Be creative. Now
bye." *Click*! I was staring at the phone like; *did she
just hang up on me*? My first reaction was to get
mad but then I felt proud. The fact that she hung

up without giving me play by play instructions told me that she trusted me to handle this. I was determined not to let her down. Our family's name is on the line and now I have to do what I have to do....bottom line.

I left the room to get the wheelchair I saw earlier in the hallway. The plan was to roll her right out the hospital to the car. Her face still looked perfect due to her makeup and hair. I just killed her so her body was still warm. People would probably just assume that she was asleep; however, I knew I had limited time. As I was bringing the wheelchair back into the room a petite white nurse started walking straight towards me.

"Ma'am that room is vacant. May I help you?" she asked trying to barge past me into the room. *Gasp!* I heard Kendra gasping for air as she took the pillow case off of her head while trying to get out of the hospital bed at the same time. "Oh my God, what is going on in here? Ma'am are you okay?" The nurse asked loudly as she ran to help Kendra take the pillow case off of her head. The nurse went to hit the red button above the bed on the wall. I tackled her to the floor before she could do it. Then Kendra jumped off the bed and started stomping me while the nurse and I were on the floor.

"Bitch you killed my sister then tried to kill me! I'm going to beat your ass before I call the police," she said as she grabbed me by my hair to get me off of the nurse.

"Run nurse. Go get help!" she yelled, as she held my hair so tight I thought my entire scalp was going to come off. The nurse got up and started to run for the door. I heard the door open, and then I saw the nurse hydroplane backwards, back into the room, hitting her head hard on the hospital room floor. Blood started pouring from the womb on the back of her head. I looked at the direction of the door and saw Dream standing there. At that point, she noticed Kendra holding me by the hair and charged her. We both stomped the shit out of Kendra until she was motionless. I checked her pulse this time to confirm that she was dead.

"I'm so sorry, Dream, that I keep placing you in these situations. Auntie doesn't know what is going on in our family right now," I said hugging her.

"It's okay Auntie. I love you all and I know you would do the same for me." We put the nurse's body in the bathroom shower to give us more time to get out of there. Since we were in a vacant room and no one saw us, there should be no way to connect us, I thought. We rolled Kendra out as planned and headed to the lake to meet Adrianna and Diamond.

CHAPTER 11

Nina

I looked at my phone and noticed it was only two o'clock pm. I had missed calls and texts from Malcolm. My father came in the house looking happier than usual. However, the change of my mother's facial expression told me there was a major flag on the play. Daddy was whistling taking off his coat to hang it up on the coat rack. I figured he must have put money on the golf game this time and won! My father was so unusually happy that he didn't even notice my mother's heart go cold or he just didn't care. Then I noticed he didn't have on golf clothes. He had on church clothes.

"Daddy, you went to church?"

"Yes, baby girl," he said, taking his hat and scarf off. I shot a look at Mama asking with my eyes why didn't she go too. Daddy picked up on my vibe and replied, "She hasn't been to Church in three weeks. When she said she wasn't going again this morning I decided to go to represent the family." Mama got up to get something from the kitchen. I was like a little girl all over again with hope in my eyes that God was working on my daddy. I ran over to him and hugged him. I thought, maybe he would change his behavior towards me now that God is in his heart again.

"You have mail Sweetie." Mama said, handing Daddy the yellow envelope.

"Woman, what I tell you about opening up my mail? I know I've told you time and - " Daddy was interrupted by the shock of the contents that were in the envelope.

"What did the Lord tell your gay ass about opening up to men – especially married men?" Mama said with a stone cold face. My father dropped the envelope and all of the pictures poured out onto the floor. My heart dropped. The pictures were Daddy and Pastor Leon having sex at the church and at the country club in the restroom. The pictures indicated the affair was ongoing for quite some time – over a year! No wonder he stopped going to the church. Oh my God! No wonder Mama stopped going. She had to have just found out.

I'd heard them arguing but couldn't make out anything. It was as if my life was just taken from me. I saw Mama all in his face yelling, "I knew it! I knew it! I knew it! The moment you told me that you were going to church out of nowhere after I told you Pastor Leon came out to the congregation about being gay that was the reason you stopped going when the rumors came out last year. If anything that would make any real man stay away. But nooooo, your gay ass just had to go claim your man huh?" Daddy was steaming mad and looked at me with embarrassment all in his face.

"I'm not gay! These photos are photoshopped," he said, picking up some of the photos. He lit the living room fireplace and started picking up more of the photos to toss them in to burn.

However, Mama started picking the pictures up too saying, "I'm going to blast you and him at church next Sunday by showing everyone these pictures. You cheated me out of all my youthful years! I can't believe that I believed in you! My father tried to tell me that under all those muscles that you had too much sugar in your tank. You are just a thumb in the bootyhole gay ass nigga!" She was so hurt. Anyone who witnessed it would've said they saw anger; but hurt, disappointment, brokenness, and shame filled the room. Everything after that statement went so fast and was like a bad horror movie. Daddy picked up one of my honors awards and started bashing Mama's head in. Blood splattered everywhere and I was frozen.

I couldn't even move. When he finally stopped hitting her, he fell to his knees and started cuddling her. He started singing to her their favorite love song as he rubbed his fingers through her hair. Moments later he and I both came out of shock when my phone rang. He ran towards the front hallway closet. When I remembered what was in there I went after him. "Daddy Noooooo!"

"I'm sorry baby girl. Just know I'm proud of you. I love you", he said.

POW! The gun went off! With one shot he was down. The next thing I remember was the ambulance coming and the medic saying that he was still breathing and that if we hurry to the hospital he might be able to make it. The medic pronounced my mother DOA. I don't even remember the ambulance ride. On the other hand, I do remember the doctor saying that he was sorry for my loss and that they did everything that they could do. I had immediately felt ill to my stomach. I pushed the doctor out of my way and went to the restroom to throw up.

I updated Malcolm via text. I needed him now more than ever. A fuck partner can't help you when shit really hits the fan. I needed someone who I knew actually cared about me. After getting myself together, I told myself it had to be a dream and that when I walked out of the stall I would wake up. To my surprise I saw Jullian Banks talking to herself. I immediately went into detective mode. I thanked God that she was there because I could focus my attention off the bad dream that I'd just had. I found myself not asking her the tough questions that needed to be asked. Hell, I didn't even introduce myself. I was off and rightfully so. After she told me that her father died I decided to just question her another day. It would've been cruel to question her about Chantal being missing and her father hadn't even turned cold yet. We heard a scream down the hallway. When Jullian opened the door Malcolm was on the other side waiting for me with the prettiest bouquet of white roses. I didn't want to blow his cover so I slid out behind Jullian and said, "Nice flowers." That was my way of saying thank you.

CHAPTER 12

Diamond

When I got to the gift shop I saw the most beautiful bouquet of white roses in a gorgeous unique crystal cut vase with a pale pink note from the sender placed perfectly within the roses sitting on the reserved shelf to be picked up. I knew then those were the flowers I wanted to give to Adrianna but I looked around and didn't see any more of them. A little panic sunk in my body as I saw the clerk's face turn to disappointment. I just wanted things perfect for my best friend while she was going through. "I need a dozen white roses. Ma'am, please tell me you have more of them in the back," I told the hospital gift shop owner. I laughed at myself inside for still in the *all-white everything* mode. "I'm sorry Senorita. Someone just purchased our last two bouquets of white roses just five minutes ago. They took one with them on their visit and will be taking this one with them when they leave. I do have the most beautiful White Lily flowers. Give me five minutes and I will make the bouquet for you," she said with a proud smile. I could tell that she had a kind spirit and took pride at work uplifting people's spirits who are here to visit loved ones. "Very good, I'll take them," I thankfully said, while giving her a warm smile.

While I was waiting I couldn't help but scan the store and look at all the 'congrats it's a girl' or 'a boy' balloons and stuffed animals. My heart melted. I was in my glory looking, touching, and imagining how Jay and my child would look. Then my thoughts were interrupted by Jewel's text messages that she kept sending. I didn't even bother to open the text to read them. I was so mad at her for not showing up to assist me at my book signing. I went to her name in my phone and placed her profile in *do not disturb* mode. That way I wouldn't get upset every time I saw her name pop up on my caller ID. Then I drifted back off to daydreaming. I so wish I was carrying his child. I just kept convincing myself that I couldn't be bitter because Jay told me from the beginning that he couldn't even dream of having kids. He'd already lost his childhood raising Ahmad and Jewel. I agreed early on, so it would be unfair to pressure him to change his mind now. I'm at the peak of my sales and need to be focused, so focused that I would never go back to my old life of a hustler and a Boss. Jay didn't know of my previous life but I did. Knowing that I may become well-known as an author, I would never want to be affiliated with a negative lifestyle or anyone still in that lifestyle. Therefore, I couldn't be about that life even if I wanted to. I sighed with relief that I was out of that life and I snapped back to reality when the nice lady handed me my flowers.

After breaking up the Floyd Mayweather and Pacquiao whack ass fight between the Banks sisters I received a text message from an unknown number. I opened the text and it was a picture of Jewel with tape over her mouth with an address for the caption.

You have two hours to meet me at 2637 Davidson behind the old

> *Warehouse near the railroad tracks*
> *with five hundred thousand. No cops,*
> *come alone or you know the rest!*

I froze. I could not help but to think did my past come back to haunt me. *Why would they take Jewel out of all people? Maybe they think she is the closest person to me since I don't have any kids and since Jay is a man he wouldn't be as valuable. No, they wanted Jay and I to come together to get the money. That's it!* Adrianna felt me freeze and gave me that look like, *What's up?* I whispered in her ear that we had to go. She understood that *we* meant that I needed her. Just like old times we were back in sync, just that quick.

When Adrianna got off the phone with her sister, Jullian, I couldn't help but laugh. "It hasn't been an entire hour Adrianna and not only have you told me that you have recently been involved in a murder; your sister just killed somebody who I was just standing beside minutes ago. All of you are crazy! Wow! I'm still tripping off the story you just told me about killing Chantal and now Kendra." We started laughing. We seemed to always laugh during crazy times like this because laughing is all that you could do to prevent going crazy. I caught her up regarding my life and it felt so good to share with my best friend. Adrianna noticed my facial expression change to now looking like a love sick puppy so she started laughing. She knew what I had to say next was about a man.

"I've been in a long term relationship, believe it or not." Smiling and turning her head to give me her undivided attention she said, "Whaaaaattttt! Long term? Do tell." I summarized the story of how Jay and I met and where we are now. Some parts I didn't have to go into great detail about because she knew me. I poured my heart out about me wanting a baby but tried to block it out for the greater good of my relationship. She knew then that I must really love him. If I told her I reacted a certain way, she would already know why. She was my best friend. She was the sister I never had.

When we got to the lake we immediately started digging for our old bag of guns, black on black attire, tape, handcuffs, rope and everything else we needed to make the kidnappers pay for taking Jewel.

Chapter 13

Adrianna

I didn't know Jewel but it didn't matter. Diamond was my best friend and if she loved her then I...well, I wouldn't say 'love her' but I had Diamond's back to the end. We placed everything we needed in the trunk and we were now waiting on Jullian to arrive with Kendra's body. While waiting I saw a black Charger pulling up to our spot. I smiled thinking Jullian was smart enough to bring the body in Kendra's rental car. Gangster 101 would say we had to get rid of that but Jullian had not earned her gangster certification yet. Anybody could kill anybody. Only gangsters kill and get away with it. Diamond picked up on what

I was thinking regarding the rental car and relief crossed her face.

"You taught her well, I see," she said, but soon was alarmed when another vehicle started to pull up behind Jullian. I wasn't because I recognized the white Charger as Ahmad's. As Jullian got closer I noticed Dream in the car with Jullian. "What the hell?" I asked Jullian before she could even get out the car.

"Long story but she saved my ass." I could tell by the look on her face that somehow, someway, Dream was just at the wrong place at the wrong time.

"What is Ahmad doing here?" I quickly asked to ease Diamond's thoughts.

"He is here to pick up Dream. I wanted her out of the way as soon as possible. I didn't have time to stop and since he knew where the spot was I told him to meet us here."

"How the hell does he know where our spot is? You don't even supposed to know where our spot is, Jullian," Diamond said angrily, leaning against her car like this is some bullshit. "There are way too many people here for comfort and way too many people using the word *our* regarding this location." Ahmad stuck his hand out to greet

Diamond but she gave him a look that said, *not today*. So he and Dream got into his car and left. Diamond, Jullian, and I stayed to handle the rest.

On the way out we noticed a lot of unmarked police cars passing us on the main road headed towards the lake. We weren't worried because we knew we covered our tracks well. We are pros at this. They couldn't see us anyway because Diamond had almost illegal black tint on her car. "I'm glad we got out of there in time", Jullian said.

Diamond rolled her eyes and said, "Here we go with *we* again. Let's be clear. There is no we!" Pissed all the way off this time, Jullian replied, "I gave you a pass the first time. Don't think you are going to keep getting them." Diamond starred at Jullian through her rearview mirror to look her directly in the eye, where she sat in the backseat, and said, "If I had time I would pull this car over and whip your ass with my new heels on. Now, the only reason I wouldn't put a bullet in you for that type of disrespect is because you are Adrianna's sister."

Jullian feeling very confident, because I was in the car with her, pointed her finger at Diamond's head and called her bluff saying, "Not if I put one through you first!" As we were passing one of the unmarked police cars I thought I saw the lady who I met in the ladies room earlier at the hospital. I really couldn't get a good look because Jullian's hand came up from the back seat to taunt Diamond and crossed in front of my vision as my eyes followed the car until it was completely past us. "Stop it!" I yelled. "Shit is getting out of hand. I know this is an unforeseen circumstance and all, but we are just going to have to stick together. Both of you are my sisters. Jullian you don't know Diamond like that and trust me she isn't what you want. Now Diamond, you are my best friend but if you think I'm going to let you lightweight threaten my sister, Bitch you got me fucked up. Now that we have an understanding that we are all family let's fill Jullian in on our next mission, because time is ticking."

CHAPTER 14

Nina

Until I saw Malcolm, what I witnessed at my parents' house still had not sunk in yet. I won't let it. In my mind I'm treating the incident as a new case that I just haven't started working yet. I've seen the crime scene but haven't given my thoughts to anyone yet. The Chief, dispatch, and the homicide unit have been trying to reach me for the past few hours now. They have no idea that I was actually there when the murder-suicide occurred. I haven't even told Malcolm that I was actually there.

The new system that we have at the Charlotte-Mecklenburg Police Department will highlight an address in red if a call comes from that address that is a known crime location or has been flagged in the system as a possible dangerous location. An address will also be flagged if that address matches the address of an officer. When an address is highlighted in red, dispatch sends the warning information to that police officer's mobile data terminal and to a police supervisor, then that police supervisor calls the officer on a private police channel to notify them immediately. So at this point they all think I showed up at the house after the call went out which was called in from a crime scene matching an address that I have on file in the computer database.

The team was surprised to see me join in the line of unmarked cars on the way to the lake. I put on some trap music to prevent myself from thinking about reality. I saw that Malcolm was calling but decided against answering it. I knew that he would be at the lake. I would just talk to him there. I immediately got out of the car. I gave no one time to even offer their condolences. I went straight into detective mode. Although I was handling Chantal Holmes' case as a missing person, I was still working like a homicide detective out of habit.

"Why did you text me with a '911' and this address? What are we looking for Malcolm?" I asked, interrupting him as he was showing a few officers something on a map that he had spread out on the hood of his car.

"We are looking for bodies. There may be a possibility Ms. Holmes is among the bodies. I'm looking for connection to the Loyals. Ms. Holmes' last call was made to Jullian Banks before going missing. Lady Hartwell and Sly Jones are missing and they were connected to Bossman's and West Styles' murders. I would say this is all starting to tie together very interestingly," he said out of his mouth, while his eyes asked me, *"How are you doing?"* He knew me well enough not to challenge me right now. "I knew this was something you wouldn't want to miss especially after seeing you walk out of the restroom with Jullian Banks. Did she tell you anything?" he asked, between updating me on our search plan.

"No she didn't say anything worth mentioning. I haven't properly questioned her yet, but I will tomorrow. How did you know to start searching here?" I asked, anxiously waiting.

"We found a fresh one!" I heard one of us just a few feet away from us. We walked over there ready to see what he was referring too. After digging, we all noticed that it was just freshly dug up dirt. A rookie zealously said, "A dog could have dug the dirt up."

"No, it's piled too neatly." Malcolm and I both said at the same time. We knew by the shape and size that a shovel was used.

"Someone had something buried here but not a body. The hole is too small. Let's keep looking in this wooded area before the sun goes down." He ordered them.

As everyone was digging and combing the woods Malcolm and I started to walk down the short trail that led to the lake, to talk privately. I could see the lake from where we were standing just a little bit through the trees. The closer we got to the lake I noticed its charm more and more. The lake was beautiful and calming. He grabbed my hand as soon as we were out of sight from the team to show affection. I was glad our boss, Seth, wasn't on the scene because although he knows we are just fuck buddies he wouldn't want me sexing any one in law enforcement but him. It was so secluded in this particular area which made it scary but romantic at the same time. As soon as he leaned in to kiss me, at the end of the trail I noticed tire marks leading into the water. "Malcolm, wait. Look," I said, looking down at fresh tire marks. We immediately knew we had to drain the lake and call in divers. I was excited that we found something because my numbness was starting to wear off. I contributed my numbness wearing off to being around Malcolm. The more evidence we find the more focused I will be on this case and not the other case that I haven't started yet regarding my parents. Malcolm's phone rang. I decided to make the call for the divers while he was on the phone.

When he hung up, he said, "I have to go."

"Where? What could be more important than this, especially after this big break?" He started looking nervous but before he could respond I received a text message from Seth. When I looked up to tell him I had to go he was already gone.

CHAPTER 15

Diamond

"A snake will always hiss."

"Damn it! Somebody is playing with my emotions and have me wasting my damn gas riding all around the city leaving stupid hints. Jay will be back any day now from his business trip and will notice that Jewel is gone. I can't tell him that I knew she was missing because then I will have to tell him about my past. All I can say is I haven't seen her. I just pray we get her back before he gets home. "This is horrible Adrianna!" I said, as I slid down the wall of the church sanctuary with my head down in defeat. I could tell Adrianna wasn't used to seeing me this way. Normally, I wouldn't let her but I'm not a Boss today. I'm simply a woman who doesn't want to see the man that I love hurt due to my past. I don't know who has Jewel but since they reached out to me, and by the notes that are being left addressed to me, this must be connected to my past. This is revenge. I just pray Jewel is still alive and doesn't have to pay the price.

Adrianna sat down beside me and placed my head on her chest. I felt bad because out of all days, I should be placing her head on my chest. It's amazing, all the years I've know her I have never seen Adrianna cry. Truth is I would have seen her as weak, if I did, but this time would have been an exception. We have been here the past hour decorating the sanctuary for her father's funeral. With our creative minds it looked professionally done of course. From the flowers, to the pictures, to the candles, we did it all. He was a Que so purple and gold was the color scheme throughout. Adrianna stood up and took my hand saying, "Come on bestie, let's get dressed before everyone arrives."

I was sitting on the red cloth and mahogany wood church pews thinking to myself how hungry I was. I should have eaten but I know I'm going to add at least ten pounds when I eat the church's soul food after the funeral at the repast with the family. See, I will admit what most won't which is that one of the things I look forward to during a funeral is the church ladies' food afterwards. There is always a banana pudding, some sweet tea, and some good ole golden deep fried chicken! Lord my mouth is watering. Let me stop. I was trying to hide the smirk on my face when I saw the over the top décor because I was thinking Ms. Josephine is so extra. I'm so over this funeral show already and it hasn't even started yet. Maybe my short tolerance is coming from my stomach talking. They waited three weeks to have the funeral in order for twin gold and diamond studded caskets to be specially tailored made and delivered. The other one will be used for their mother to lie beside him when she passes. They wanted their parents to be buried above the grade just like they lived their lives. Personally, I don't care what happens to my body after I'm gone. I wouldn't see, need it, nor feel it anyway.

Before going inside the church, just as the funeral procession was pulling into the church parking lot, my phone rang with an unknown number. I knew immediately by the hairs on my back that it was the kidnappers. "Oh you decided to Boss up and call directly this time instead of leaving love notes and text messages I see," I said, showing the Kidnapper that I wasn't afraid.

"Relax." I heard a woman say on the other end of the phone. I was shocked. I thought to myself you mean to tell me I'm dealing with a Bitch.

Then I replied in frustration, "This better not be over a nigga. If you already had him then you can have him -".

"Dick is the last thing on my mind. Being dick whipped is for the weak but I'll take being called a Bitch a compliment. Being one works in my favor in this line of work," the lady said in a humorous but evil tone.

"Then what is the reason for this?" I asked, hitting the steering wheel in frustration.

"Have patience and wait for instructions." *Click*

Hearing the dial tone only fueled my anger, even more, to kill whoever was behind this, without conversation. No need for dialogue. I just want to see blood. I for one don't attend funerals but Adrianna was like family to me. Trying my best not to sweat my phone for the text I actually tried to pay attention to the Pastor preach. It was crowded – full of healthcare professionals and the elite of Charlotte. Dr. Warren was still a very well respected doctor in the community although he stopped practicing. Adrianna said he still acted as a consultant for many who were currently in the field, he wrote many published medical journals, and was an online college professor to maintain his self-worth between treatments.

I kept looking at the obituary after every event to see how close we were to the funeral being over. The choir and the young boy soloist were amazing. Dream's praise dance presentation earned a standing ovation. It touched my heart but my poker face was strong. Adrianna kept trying to read my face while Dream was dancing. It was as if she knew my heart but she doubted my intention. That's the difference between Adrianna and me. I don't care what your face says. Whatever energy I pick up around you tells me everything I need to know.

The spirit in the room made me reconsider going back to church one day but not today I'm not ready to wear the Diva church hat just yet. I was so ready to go. Too many tears and sorrow. The heaviness of sadness made me feel out of place. Adrianna, Jullian, and Charisma went up to the mic to speak about how their father blessed their lives. It was a nice change of tone because their words made everyone happy.

Everything was going well until Adrianna stopped in mid-sentence with her eyes fixated on one of the guest. He was a little bit older than us, very nice looking, wearing the latest Sean John navy blue suit with expensive multi-colored brown Gators on. He had his right arm around a pregnant lady that I would assume was his wife and his other arm around a little girl that I would assume was around the age of five. The little girl had the perfect bright yellow dress on with two long silk ponytails, on each side, held by a yellow ribbon. Adrianna walked off the pulpit and out the side door that led to the restrooms and the Pastor's study. Charisma and Jullian assumed that their sister just stopped talking due to being overwhelmed speaking about their father so they continued speaking to the audience.

"Buzz"

A text message came through with an address ordering me to meet them in one hour. Attached was a p.s. note saying, "Poor timing, but money waits for no one." That told me that they were watching me. As I placed my phone back in my purse I took the safety off my nine and tapped the silencer for good luck. She needed to be ready to fire at any given time. These mutherfuckers think this is a game. Little do they know I always win.

When I looked up from my phone the pregnant lady who was sitting beside the nice looking man in the blue suit at the end of my row was headed to the restroom with her little girl. She was jumping around as if her mother had two seconds to get her to the nearest restroom or it was going to be a problem. I decided to go check on Adrianna and tell her that I had to leave. I wasn't going to tell her why because she would have left with me, unapologetically. Jullian and Charisma were now standing behind their mother who just stepped up to speak in the pulpit. They all gave me the nod to say thank you for checking on Adrianna for them when they saw me stand up. I smiled back as I was making my way down the row. The man in the navy blue suit stood up so that I could pass by. Instead of curving his pelvis back he stood there enjoying every minute of my behind rubbing past his groin area to get by. I shot him a look that said, "You have the wrong one." He just chuckled with a sinister grin. I kept going because I had less than an hour now to get to Jewel. I had to remain focus.

When I got to the back of the church I saw Adrianna and the pregnant lady talking in front of the ladies room. "Hi little one," Adrianna said, playing super happy, with a big smile, and leaning over to meet the pretty little girl at eye level as the little girl walked out of the restroom. "How old are you?"

"I'm five," the little girl said, holding up five fingers.

"Well, you are the prettiest five-year old I've ever seen," Adrianna said with joy and sadness in her voice. I assumed she was trying to mask her sadness from the funeral while talking to the little girl so I brushed it off.

"Thank you," the mother of the girl said with a proud tone and smile. You could tell she was proud of her little girl. "I am hoping for a boy this time but my husband only wants girls," the mother of the girl said rubbing her belly as she motioned to go back into the sanctuary. Before she went out the door that led into the sanctuary, she said, "I'm sorry for your loss. I didn't know him but I heard he was a good man." Adrianna awkwardly smirked and stated, "You heard that he was a good man huh." You could tell the lady became very uncomfortable at Adrianna's change in demeanor. She opened the door that led to the sanctuary and while walking out she lightly tapped the back of her little girl's back saying to her,

"Come on Adrianna. Daddy is waiting." I saw my best friend and the little girl freeze like the Statue of Liberty.

"Mama I don't want to sit beside daddy."

CHAPTER 16

Adrianna

"Rock-a-bye Baby."

"Let's go. We're on the clock." I commanded walking out the back of the church expecting Diamond to follow behind me.

Grabbing my arm to get me to stop, Diamond asked, "Who is 'we'? You are needed here. Let me handle the street," she firmly said, as if I was one of the Loyals instead of her equal. I didn't take offense because I understood that she was just trying to use her authoritarian voice to pull rank because she knew I wouldn't listen any other way. "What's up with you and that lady and how do you know that we are on the clock?" Dia asked curiously, laughing at me, as we were walking to her white Jag. I ignored her first question. I didn't have the energy to explain. I'm already drained from the funeral, no sleep all night due to running to the bathroom, and was secretly sweating the fact that Jackson didn't show up because I had something to tell him that was important.

"Diamond, you had the eye of the Tiger in your eyes after you checked your phone. I was watching you from the pulpit just like I was watching everything else. So how long do we have to get there?" I asked.

"Now we have forty five minutes but it's only fifteen minutes away so no problem," Dia said looking at her MK watch as we turned around the building to go out the front parking lot.

As we were pulling out I noticed the pregnant lady and her daughter rushing to her car. Dia and I immediately knew something was off so we pulled up to her. "Ma'am, are you okay?" I asked.

"Adrianna, put your seat belt on," she said hurriedly, trying to ignore me while getting into the car to put on her seatbelt.

Then I heard a man's voice yell, "Bitch I'll kill you if you take my kids!" He was so driven to stop her that he didn't even see us in the car beside her.

Diamond put the car in reverse to pull out the parking space saying, "Oh no. I don't get in domestic disputes. What woman doesn't know her man ain't shit after the first child. She's pregnant again so clearly she likes it so I love it. We have to go."

Before I could tell Diamond to hold up, the lady jumped out the car like a Mama Bear and yelled, "Not if I kill you first you nasty mutherfucker! Adrianna show him your hands!" She grabbed little Adrianna's hands to show him what was on them.

The little girl started to cry saying, "I didn't tell our secret Daddy."

There was blood on them. Immediately Diamond put the car back in park and said, "Oh hell no!"

The lady got up in his face and said, "We all know the only way she can have blood on her hands after using the restroom is if she has blood in her panties. Now you are going to bleed blood as soon as I tell my father." My head started spinning and all I could see was red. Diamond and I jumped out the car at the same time. When he saw me he acted like he saw a ghost. I guess he expected me to still be inside the church.

"Long time no see Donald. I see you haven't changed much," I said, motioning my head towards his daughter's hands. I wanted to kill him right then and there but his daughter was looking and the lady was pregnant.

Diamond calmly interrupted and directly told the lady, "Lady you have five seconds to decide if you want this nightmare to be over permanently. If you do your wish is granted." The lady saw Diamond's gun slightly hidden to her side. I could tell Diamond was set to go. She saw this as an "if A then B" situation. He was so full of himself that he didn't even notice the gun or that Diamond was not playing with him. You could tell he held no value to women nor even been in a presence of a strong one because if he did he would have recognized that Diamond wasn't the one. I guess because she wasn't barking and was so calm that he wasn't scared. Little did he know, when you are dealing with a woman of intellect, the calm is always before the storm.

"Bitch you are not going to do anything to me. You probably wouldn't even bust a grape in your pretty all white. Mind your business," Donald said, dismissing Diamond. Oooooweeeee, the lovely Adrianna Banks, you sure as hell turned out to be just as beautiful as I thought you would be. You see, I named my daughter after you." The lady threw up in disgust. You could tell that she put two and two together and couldn't believe she married a molester and a rapist. He didn't even acknowledge her being sick. He just continued. "I should have waited a few years so that I could have married you instead," he said, reaching to touch my romance curls that fell past my shoulders.

I immediately became that little girl again in my own yellow dress at his house. I couldn't even move. Before he actually touched my hair the lady looked back at her little girl and saw the fear in her face and said, "Do it!"

As soon as she covered her daughter's eyes Diamond dropped him with her silencer. He fell to the church parking lot payment but was still alive. Diamond normally shoots one shot to the head. She handed me the gun and said, "The final shot to the head is yours sis. Make it quick." It was the first time I heard my heart beating through my chest before a kill. "We have to go," she snapped, getting back into her car to wait for me. I stepped over him looking at him gargle blood trying to plead for his life with his eyes. I felt nothing but hate for him.

"This is for every little girl who couldn't defend herself against you and for the child that's in me that will never have to deal with you again." I spit in his face then I rocked him to sleep.

"I'm a Boss and a Boss is always trained to go." I said jumping back into the car after I handed the lady ten thousand out of Diamond's stash in the trunk with a promise to send her another thirty for her and her kids later in the week. I knew seeing the father of her child get murdered before her eyes had to be bittersweet. By the look in her eyes we could tell that she knew it was for the best. Some might have wondered why I didn't just call the police. My answer to that is that some justice is best served cold.

During the first few minutes of the ride we didn't speak a word. I was glad that she got back into the car and didn't hear my final words to Mr. Donald. I wanted to talk to her about me being three weeks pregnant but then she really wouldn't let me ride. I'll tell her later after the storm is over. She would look at me as another responsibility instead of her equal. I can't have that. Plus, I know it would be a bitter pill for her to swallow considering she decided to put her dream of having a baby on hold for Jay. Diamond knew that my head was still racing from today's events so she decided to give me a moment. I knew she was worried about Jewel more than she let on so I decided to Boss up to show her that I'm on a thousand with her. "After we take them out I want you to meet someone special in my life. His name is Jackson. Trust me you will approve."

Diamond let out a half grin and said, "He already has my approval if you are introducing him to me because I know if he was anything less than stellar we wouldn't even be having this conversation. Was he at the funeral?"

"Unless he arrived late after we went to the back, I didn't see him. I, myself, thought that was strange. He came up to the hospital to show love which really won my family over. It's the first time I felt magic when a man touched me since Boss. I mean Darnelle was good in bed but I've only felt magic with Boss and Jackson. We should all go out and double date with you and Jay. I think I'm falling in love Dia." I went on and on. I told her about how we met and each encounter, and then Diamond started teasing me for cheesing like a school girl by pinching my cheeks. In that moment I almost forgot about what had just happened back at the church.

Just as the warehouse got in eye view Diamond said, "I have orders to go in alone. Keep the car running. If I'm not back in ten leave me."

I threw my head back in shock and snapped back, "Leave you? That's never going to happen!"

She jumped out of the car, putting her head back in the window and said, "This is a different type of beast. We don't know who we are dealing with this time around and because of that we don't have time to plan a way out. Normally we know the location or the strategy. This is a blind spot this time. Let's not even mention Jewel is in there unarmed. If I lose her Jay would just die." Her voice became so weak and soft when she uttered her last sentence. I could feel the love she had for that man. I knew then that he was different for her. He had her heart although she didn't want to admit it. I grabbed her hand and assured her with my words.

"I have your back, Diamond, just like you have mine. Today was just another day in our line of work. No need to protect me Dia."

She gently grabbed my hand and said, "I'm not necessarily just protecting you." Then she placed her hand on my stomach. "I'm protecting the baby."

CHAPTER 17

Nina

I pulled up to the warehouse wondering why Seth would want me to meet him here. Perhaps he wanted to talk to me about my parents' death face-to-face outside of the office or without other officers around. I could appreciate that. Eventually, I would have to talk to someone about it so it might as well be him. He told me to come down a side road that would lead me to the back door in order for me to avoid the front. I thought that was strange but he is the boss so I followed orders.

I parked right beside his car in the back so I knew he was inside. Yet, something didn't feel right in my spirit. The warehouse was dark, dry, and gloomy when I entered. I pulled out my nine and flashlight as I walked down the hallway leading to an open space. "Hi Seth. Are you here?" I called out but received no answer. As I turned the corner to the open space I immediately knew I had walked into the lion's den. I noticed Seth and some lady in the latest Giorgio Armani cashmere dress from this season's runway. She looked like Naomi Campbell's "Boss Lady" character that she plays on Empire, leaning against the desk, apparently waiting on me. She was most definitely a Boss. "Lower your weapon Nina," he said motioning with his hand for me to lower it. Then he ushered me over to them. I did as I was told but I didn't trust the piercing stare in the unknown woman's eyes when they appeared from the Roberto Cavalli shades she was wearing. They were deadly and could kill, if they could, with one look. Then my world went black.

When I came through, groggily, I had no idea how much time had passed. All I had on was my bra and jeans because my mouth was gagged with my blouse. My head was pounding. "You haven't been out long. No more than five minutes at the most," I heard a woman say calmly to the right of me. I turned in the direction of her calm voice and when my vision became clear I noticed how stunningly beautiful she was. She was calm but she had revenge in her eyes. I couldn't help but to wonder why her mouth wasn't gagged like mine. I know we haven't been here long for more reasons than one. I could smell my fresh deodorant. I didn't have to use the bathroom and my Victoria's Secret lip gloss I applied earlier that today was still popping on my lips.

"I bet you are wondering why my mouth isn't gagged. I am too. And his mouth isn't either," she said, nodding in the direction to the left of me.

"Malcolm!" I tried to say, but it came out muffled through my shirt. He was waking up and starting to realize what was happening. He had blood all on his deep silver dress shirt with a black left eye. He could tell by my eyes I was yelling, "I'm glad you are here! I meant I'm not glad you are here but you know what I mean. Do you know what is going on? Why is Seth doing this?" I asked him through my eyes and body language, as if he would know.

He cleared his throat and said, "They drugged us but I'm going to get us out of here. Who are you?" he asked, looking at the stunningly beautiful lady.

"Who am I?" she questioned back as if he should've known not to ask her. Her face looked confused, sad, angry, and hurt all at the same time. Then the room became silent. It was like the calm before the storm type of quiet. Then I heard, POW! POW! POW! POW! POW! Before I could hear another sound I blacked out again.

CHAPTER 18

Diamond

The gunshots and two thumps, indicating bodies dropping, were music to my ears because I knew that my girl Adrianna was in the building. I was sort of jealous I couldn't pop off with her because our kidnappers knocked me over the head and took my nine. I got myself free from the ropes within the first few minutes using my ring razor. I didn't want to draw any attention until Adrianna got here. I knew if I didn't come out in a few minutes that she would come in unloading clips so I played it safe. Adrianna busted in the door wearing a navy blue Yankee fitted hat with a matching bandana over her face. All I could see were a little bit of her gorgeous green eyes and her eyes said *I am not playing any games*! "Here," Adrianna said, as she winked at me while throwing me my gun. It felt so good to be back in control holding my diamond studded gun handle shining like I just got it. It will never tell how many bodies it has on it.

Thirty seconds later I heard, "Malcolm! Malcolm!" the pretty brown skinned lady screamed as she ran over to assist him. "Help me get him up! I think he has passed out! What happened when I was passed out?" she demanded to know. I was about to fill her in but that's when I noticed her police badge that fell out of her pants as she was trying to get him to his feet. I immediately drew my gun on her.

"You're fucking my man ….and you're a cop too!?" I demandingly asked. He started to come through from me knocking him out a few seconds ago. The lady cop looked so confused. I had to admit I was confused too. Earlier, I knocked her out first, and then I had knocked Jay out after he tried to explain. He opened his eyes slightly and saw me holding the gun on the lady cop. All he could see was a masked lady holding the gun on him. I noticed Adrianna standing in the doorway with her gun halfway lowered and by her stance

I could tell she was in shock as she watched the lady cop help Jay get up.

"What the hell is going on Jay?" I coldly demanded.

Something was off with him. He wasn't ...himself. Trying to stand up by himself with his hands held up pleading for neither of us to shoot, he said softly, "Diamond, babe I ...."

POW!

All of a sudden Adrianna pulled the trigger and put a bullet in his right shoulder causing him to fall back down against the wall in eminent pain. My life flashed in front of me. For the first time in a long time I had mixed emotions. I'm either in or out. I either love you or I don't. I'm either done dealing with you or I'm ride or die. Although I was going to make Jay pay for cheating, I still needed answers before I killed him. "What the hell are you doing Adrianna!!!?," I yelled, losing focus on the pretty lady cop I had my gun on. It was as if Adrianna didn't even hear me. The lady cop noticed I was distracted by love and took advantage by twisting my arm causing me to release the gun. She grabbed the gun and placed it to my head in less than one second.

Adrianna immediately snapped back and put her gun on the cop.

"Lower your weapon Adrianna!" the cop ordered. Adrianna took off her hat letting her soft curls fall and snatched down her bandana. She was beautifully gangster.

"No Bitch, you lower yours," Adrianna demanded with no fear in her heart.

"How does she know your name, Adrianna?" I asked, trying to breathe as the cop squeezed tighter on the choke hold she had on me. I didn't know what was going on but on my Mama when I got free it was over for her!

"This is the cop that has been investigating my family. Her name is Detective Ross. Funny, because just a few minutes ago, while waiting outside, I got a phone call from an insider informing me that we are under investigation. They literally just sent me a picture of you, beautiful, just in case I ran into you but coincidentally I already had at the hospital." Considering the timing of it all Adrianna couldn't help but chuckle while making that statement. Adrianna walked closer to the cop causing the cop to place the hold she already had on me tighter. "I'm only going to warn you once," Adrianna fearlessly warned her knowing in her heart that she was going to offer a kill shot as soon as she could. I could feel the Detective shaking her head trying to come out of the fog she was in from the knockout I gave her. It was causing her to lose focus which caused her to hold on to me even tighter due to fear of losing control of the situation. As Adrianna was moving forward, backing Detective Ross and I in the corner, I was cheering for Adrianna to take a headshot as soon as I was able to move my head just a little to the right. However, due to the tight hold she had on me, that was impossible because Detective Ross knew that once Adrianna had a shot it was over for her. I could see Adrianna's finger on the trigger looking dead into the cop's eyes staring her down like a Boss. I had to admit, I was a proud sister in this moment. Then I saw the shift in Adrianna's eyes as she was calculating if she could take the shot. In my head I was thinking, *Noooo! Wait until I'm able to move my head. I'm not ready yet.* Then I heard a shot.

POW!

Gunfire was starting not to be my best friend.

CHAPTER 19

Nina

If these Hoes think for one second I'm not walking out of here alive they have another thing coming. My mind was racing. My heart has never beaten so fast. These women were assassins, highly trained, and gangster with it. What made them even more deadly was their beauty which could distract the enemy if you're not careful. Today, it's either them or me and it sure as hell isn't going to be me. I wasn't in the mood for making arrest. My eyesight was blurry. I could tell Adrianna was trained so my first shot had to be a perfect shot. I couldn't leave room for a retaliation shot. That may cost me my life. They shot my Malcolm, Seth set us up, and I have a feeling since I really don't know what is going on that I might not be able to prove my story. "Fuck!!!" I yelled. This situation couldn't be any worse. It seemed like yelling only caused my vision to worsen. I could tell they knew I was backed up in a corner and by the way I cursed they knew, somehow, I was in a bad situation.

"Who is he to you?" Adrianna asked me, nodding her head over to Malcolm, who was in so much pain from his gunshot. He was trying to apply pressure but blood was everywhere. Seeing him in so much pain made me realize I've been a fool to push him away. It's okay to guard your heart but don't build the wall so high that you can't even see the right man on the other side. I felt tears forming when I realized how much he meant to me.

"He is a Homicide Detective ....my friend........and the man I just realized that I love."

POW!

Adrianna shot him again, without even taking her eyes off of me, in his left shoulder this time. "Adrianna! Chill!" Diamond yelled as I tried to squeeze the life out of her, just a little, with my grip with one hand and pointing my gun at Adrianna with the other hand.

Crossing both arms across his chest, trying to use the right hand to stop the bleeding of the left shoulder and vice versa, Malcolm tried to speak through his pain, pleading, "Adrianna look at me! Look at me dammit!" Adrianna acted as if she didn't hear him but her ear was opened to his words. My vision was getting worse. I was fighting hard to shake it but I felt like I was in a cloud of haze. All of a sudden I heard Malcolm start explaining himself to these women as if he needed to.

"This started as an undercover assignment for all the bodies you two have on you from being in the game. We still don't know who killed Boss, West, nor Lady. Sly, Diamond's brother is missing. Chantal, your father's ex-girlfriend, is missing. Then on the way here I got a phone call stating the hospital found the body of a nurse that was conveniently killed a few rooms down from your father's hospital room during the time all of you were up there. Kendra had an appointment at the police station today to go over some facts regarding her twin sister Chantal's case, but all of a sudden she is no longer answering any phone calls and missed her appointment. I bet neither Diamond nor you know anything about that huh? Shit!" he screamed in pain while holding the shoulder with the most excruciating pain before he continued. "Nina, Detective Ross here, is investigating your family friend, Chantal, who conveniently came up missing after being seen with the Banks family. We don't know how you all are doing it but we are one step closer. We're draining the lake as we speak," he said in a, *we caught them voice.* "I thought I was up here on a lead from Seth. I remember walking in the warehouse seeing him standing next to notorious Lady Red. Last time I saw her she was on the FBI's Most Wanted list. Next thing I know I woke up in a room with you two," he said, referring to Diamond and Nina. "Nina, obviously Seth is up to no good and we are just collateral damage some kind of way. I haven't figured it out yet. Everything happened too fast. He must have knocked me out. All I know is that things weren't supposed to turn out like this."

"Where is Jewel?" Diamond managed to say between shallow breaths. As soon as she asked that questioned Seth came through the door holding Jewel hostage with a gun held to her head.

"The reunion is over. Everyone put your guns down," Seth said with confidence, now that he was running the show. Adrianna and I reluctantly put our guns down knowing that we were not a match for his gun, he had Jewel who looked terrified, and even if we did shoot him he was bound to take one of us out with him. In that moment we knew it was us against him.

CHAPTER 20

Diamond

Nina realized that Officer Seth was dirty and in order for her to survive she needed all hands on deck…even mine. She released me. I started to knock her ass out again but we needed her too…for now anyway. I was so happy to see Jewel alive that I didn't know what to do. She looked so scared but clean. Her hair was even still on fleek. "Go over there and pick up their guns," Seth commanded as he pushed Jewel in the back towards us. "Then bring them back to me." When Jewel got close to me I opened my arms to hug her. I felt so bad for being mad at her for not showing up at the book signing. I didn't know she was kidnapped. She hugged me, kissed me on the cheek, and then put my gun that she picked up from the ground to my head. Seth sinisterly started laughing.

"Do you ladies get it now? Diamond and Adrianna, we lured you here so that Lady Red and Jewel could seek her revenge on you two for their sister's death.

"Who the fuck is her sister?" I demanded.

"Lady. She was one of your Loyals but I guess she wasn't loyal just like my man Malcolm," he said, laughing at how Malcolm's body was slumped over knowing that one of us did it. "I planted Jewel with Malcolm to play his sister as he played boyfriend to Diamond thinking he was working on a case. What he didn't realize was that he was working for me and I was reluctantly working for Lady Red. Thank you, Adrianna, for solving my problem. I might just give you a quick death as a thank you. We used Malcolm's personal knowledge of you two to help us lure you here. We had to learn your weaknesses and strengths before coming after you. You two are cold blooded murderers. We could have taken you out but Lady Red and Jewel wanted you to suffer first. I called Malcolm here because he was trying to fuck Nina knowing I was fucking her.

I loved you Nina and this is the thanks I get. I guess you were simply going to fuck your way up the corporate ladder, huh?"

"Fuck you Seth!" I could see the spit coming out of Nina's mouth when she said it. She was on a thousand. She was madder than I've ever seen a woman before. That level of anger was unbeknown to women like us in the game. Adrianna and I normally don't get mad. We get even. "Seth you know I just lost both of my parents today in a murder-suicide so I could care less than a fuck about your feelings towards me." She walked two steps towards him knowing that he wouldn't shoot her just yet. The man just confessed his love to her. If anything she would be the last person in the room that he would kill if he kills her. "After what I witnessed today I don't even care about life so do what you must do Seth. You are a fuck boy and the only thing fuck boys are good for is a good fuck." You could tell by his facial expression and sadness in his eyes that he was hurt. She paused and looked at him with disgust in her eyes and said, "I would have never loved you." Then she spit the biggest hurl of spit in his face.

Nina rushed him attempting to take away gun while biting the arm holding the gun like an attack dog. As soon as we saw the distraction I stomped on Jewel's foot while grabbing her arm with the gun holding it up towards the ceiling. I pressed her finger on the trigger to let off shots trying to unload the clip or buy Adrianna enough time to grab her gun. Just as expected Adrianna went right into beast mode when the distraction took place, picking her gun up from the ground and shooting Jewel in the head killing her instantly.

Blood was shooting from Seth's arm. He had no choice but to drop the gun out of pain. She grabbed it and held it on him. They were eye to eye. "Oh, I'm under arrest now beautiful. Who do you think they are going to believe? I would tell them that you lost your marbles after your parents' deaths today. First, I'm going to get one last nut. Tell me, Nina, should I come in your pussy or in your mouth? Then I'm going to bury you next to your fucked up parents."

CLACK! CLACK! CLACK! CLACK! CLACK! She just snapped. Seth never saw it coming and I never saw the next death coming either.

Adrianna looked at Jay, Malcolm, or whatever his name is and said, "Diamond, meet my Baby's Daddy, Jackson." I was lost for words. Jay's eyes flew open in shock. I think he forgot he was even shot when he heard Adrianna's revelation.

"POW!" Adrianna took Jay out with one head shot.

Chapter 21

Nina

"9-1-1….What is the address of your emergency? Do you need fire, medic, or police?"

"This is…." I made up in my mind to tell the truth, the whole truth, and nothing but the truth but the two small red dots that suddenly appeared, one on my chest and the other on my head, caused me to rethink my current situation. I tried to dial 9-1-1 on my cell that I got back off of Seth's body while Adrianna and Diamond were distracted by the revelation that we were all screwing the same man, before his untimely death. I looked directly at the two shooters, as if they weren't pointing guns, showing compliance.

They knew that I had a change of heart by the current expression on my face.

As the operator kept repeating, "Fire, police or medic?" I pressed the end button on the phone disconnecting from the 9-1-1 operator.

I kept thinking about all the bodies lying in pools of fresh blood. I knew that I could become an accomplice to a crime and not just any crime, murder. Not just any murder, the murder of my captain, the man I used to sleep with, and he is so sadistic there is no telling what he planted for me to go down just in case the tables turned. I kept thinking to myself, *how did I get here? Why me? Can I even trust these people? Can I even trust myself now?*

Knowing I was screwed either way, I reluctantly said, "You two get the legs and I'll get the arms."

"We are going to have to burn the body this time. We can't leave any room for mistakes," one of the shooters said.

I replied sending a deadly look, "No shit Sherlock. If we leave it up to any of you, we all will be in jail."

"You're right. We can't even argue with you about that," one said, while the other agreed nodding their heads. To my surprise they both started laughing but then the laughing abruptly stopped.

Adrianna "Free at Last"

"This breeze feels so good off the ocean doesn't it little mama," Diamond said, rocking baby Jada in her arms as if she were hers instead of being her Goddaughter. Jada had some features of her father, Jackson, but she was mostly me. She got my green eyes, lips, and complexion but has her father's nose. Diamond wrapped her up in the perfect pink and white Chanel baby blanket. You could tell my baby was exhausted from all the attention she was getting and I loved every moment of it. It was the perfect day on the beach and we were blessed to have the entire family here with no worries.

"The food is almost done. Everyone go wash your hands," Mama said yelling from the grill as her new man kissed her on the cheek. I was so happy to see her happy again. I looked over at Charisma and Rashad who seemed more in love than ever. Their family was beautiful. Jordan was getting taller every second. Charisma said Rashad wanted another child but Charisma said that she was done. Somehow I didn't believe her. Then my eyes softened as I saw Dream setting the outside table on the deck for us. We all started laughing as her Gucci flop hat flew off her head into the pool. Mama rushed over to her like her life depended on it and fixed Dream's hair and checked up on her makeup as if she was getting ready for a family photoshoot. My mother could be extra at times. Then I looked at Jullian who was smiling from ear to ear and blushing from whomever she was video chatting with. It better be a nigga because I can still taste the residue from her and Chantal.

My thoughts were interrupted by Diamond, asking proudly, "Now you see why I had to do what I had to do?" as she gently placed Jada in my arms. "We have to always protect the family. Family always comes first. We can't afford to leave any rock unturned. So, I had to do what I had to do. If I didn't there was a chance the entire case wouldn't have gone away. Leave no witnesses. It's just the way it is. I hope you are not still mad at me, Adrianna."

I gave her a slight grin and assured her. "No I'm not mad. I never was mad at you. I was just disappointed that we had to kill the same person who saved our lives."

"No, she saved our lives to save her life," Diamond quickly cut her eyes at me to make sure I got the point. "I do wish things could have been different because Nina might have been a rider if she wasn't a cop." We laughed at the notion of a three man team. We both knew that we were more than enough and another person would be way too much for this earth.

After saying grace over the food, the handsome Ahmad showed up. He and Dream were going strong and they made each other happy. Ahmad was still mourning the loss of his brother but will never know our role in his death.

QUESTIONS

1. What do you believe the title of Adrianna's book would be if she wrote one?
2. Which death surprised you the most?
3. How do you feel about the death of Mr. Banks and which child took his death the hardest?
4. Who do you believe Malcolm loved the most and why?
5. Do you think Ahmad and Dream will survive when she goes off to Harvard?
6. Do you think it was fair for Charisma to keep her father's illness a secret from her sisters?
7. Who do you think would win in a fight between Jullian and Diamond?
8. What were your thoughts about Donald appearing at the funeral?
9. Why do you believe the last chapter is titled "Free at Last"?
10. Which character(s) would you like to see play a major role if book three were to be written?

Printed in the United States
By Bookmasters